MURDER
IN THE
STEENS

To Andy, Kinnore,
Steven & Scotty

Thanks for
coming to my

book launch.

Ron Covell

Books in the Thomas Martindale Series

Murder at Yaquina Head

Dead Whales Tell No Tales

Lights, Camera, MURDER!

Murder Below Zero

Searching for Murder

Descent into Madness

Yaquina White

Murder in E-flat Major

A THOMAS MARTINDALE MYSTERY

MURDER IN THE STEENS

RON LOVELL

FIRST Edition
Penman Productions, Gleneden Beach, Oregon
Copyright © 2012 by Ronald P. Lovell

Printed in the United States of America
Library of Congress Control Number: 2011940723
ISBN: 978-0-9767978-8-3

Cover and book designer: Liz Kingslien
Editor: Mardelle Kunz
Cover photo of Kiger Gorge by Dennis Wolverton, denniswolverton@comcast.net
Horse photo: © Maria Itina | Dreamstime.com
Back cover photo of Ron Lovell at Steens Mountain
by Denny Douglass

Penman
PRODUCTIONS

P.O. Box 400, Gleneden Beach, Oregon 97388
www.martindalemysteries.com

Acknowledgments for
Murder in the Steens

To Barbara—One of my oldest friends,
without whose help this story
could not have been written.
Thank you.

With deepest thanks for the help of:

Bill & Cathy Dickson
Denny & Ruth Douglass
Trina Hutchins
Bob Webster
Jay & Becky White
Dennis Wolverton
Russ Wright

WE STAND AT THE TOP OF THE CIRQUE, *looking north down the lovely swing to the left made by the glacier as it carved the Kiger Gorge. The bottom, where a lovely stream flows, is nearly half a mile below us. Beavers live there, and deer can be seen feeding along the canyon face and in the meadows made by the beavers.... A number of old-timers have mentioned the Indian artifacts lying about in the head of Kiger Gorge prior to the time the soil was disturbed by domestic livestock and erosion covered much of the bottom. All of the mountain gorges must have afforded excellent summering areas for the Indians. Fish and game were abundant and there was excellent graze for their bands of ponies.*

— E. R. JACKMAN, *Steens Mountain: In Oregon's high desert country*

CHAPTER 1

Spring Term 2009

I HAD A TINY BIT OF STAGE FRIGHT as I put my hand on the door-knob and prepared to enter—I hadn't been in a classroom for over three years. It seemed strange because I had been teaching at Oregon University for twenty years and had talked to hundreds, maybe thousands of students during my time on the faculty. For the most part, students were a receptive audience and listened to what I had to say about the field they wanted to enter—journal-ism—because I knew more than they did, of course, having spent years "in the trenches" of a fascinating and rewarding career.

But that was when I started. My experience then was as fresh as the pinstriped suits—my "New York suits" I called them—that I wore my first few years. The suits made me stand out from my less-experienced colleagues in the department. In later years, I dressed more casually, although I always wore a dress shirt and a tie. I did not want to be like "one of the kids," as a younger, jean-clad instructor once told me he aspired to be. I needed a bit of authority, and the dress shirt and tie gave me that from the moment I walked in the door. I could bolster the right to be authoritative in the way I handled my subject matter and the atmosphere in the classroom as the term progressed.

But that was all in the past. And here I was, many years later with a nervous stomach. I knew the feeling had less to do with the undergraduates awaiting my arrival inside the classroom than with my tenuous status in the department and the university itself. For the past few years, I had been on leave without pay, a perk the academic world bestows on tenured faculty members, which allows them to keep their positions while they pursue other interests. In my case, I had taken the extended leave in order to write a book.

At least that was the official reason; the real reason was more complicated.

Several years ago, I was arrested for murdering someone. I was innocent and only spent a night in the local jail. In fact, the person I was arrested for killing was not even dead. But all of that seemed to matter little to some of the people in my department. They sniped and sniggered behind my back and even expressed reservations about having me as a colleague.

The chairman of my department and officials higher up in the university hierarchy supported me fully, so my job was never in jeopardy. My reputation and the tenure system also protected me. But I still felt more than a bit paranoid when I was on campus. Were people talking behind my back? Would my career continue to flourish the way it had before?

Adding to that was my involvement in bringing to justice the leader of a Mexican drug gang and a group of Islamic terrorists—not the normal job description for a college journalism professor—which put me in a kind of danger that the tenure system could not protect me from. At times, I could not concentrate on my work or even eat. It was hard to get a good night's sleep. At one point, I even feared that I was suffering from the posttraumatic stress disorder experienced by men and women who had been in war. I was constantly worried about my safety and found that I could not function normally.

I was able to keep writing, however, and the financial success of my book *The Cocaine Trail* helped put my mind—and my bank account—at ease. Also, the various bad guys were finally arrested or killed, so I was no longer in physical danger.

As these problems disappeared, I became bothered by my status at the university. My rather sensational story had faded considerably, as most stories do in this environment of 24/7 news, but I still felt uneasy.

But these memories faded, and I was back at the door of the classroom, my hand on the knob. I was going to give teaching another try. I felt I owed it to an institution that had been very good to me. And besides, I was too young to retire and the cachet of a professorship rounded out my resume nicely.

The man who first hired me, Lloyd Quimby, had died several years before, after my "incident." He was a great chairman who had built journalism into a gem of a department that catered to students and focused on preparing them for meaningful careers. His specialty was photojournalism, and a number of his students had gone on to land good jobs in magazines and newspapers. The department was always weaker on the writing side, largely due to the lack of experience in some of the older faculty—the people who I always felt disparaged me so. My leaving had been a blow to the department and to Lloyd, but I couldn't control what had happened to me.

Lloyd's replacement as chairman, Randy Webb, was also a photographer. He and I had worked together years ago in a bizarre incident at the coast where a hapless country sheriff had tried to blow up a dead whale. I had made sure that Randy was on hand to record the chaos and mess that resulted; his photos had earned him extra money . . . and a bit of fame.

Webb had called me at Thanksgiving last year to see if I would come back part-time to teach a graduate seminar on book writing. "You can get your feet wet during the spring term and see if you want to teach more next year," he had said. "Tom, I really need you to do this. All the retirements and Lloyd's death have really hurt us."

I could not refuse him or his request that I also conduct a one-credit course about careers in mass media, the not-so-new buzzword that was being used to describe our business these days.

So . . . I pulled the classroom door open and stepped inside. I always did this kind of dramatic entrance on the first day of class to make a firm impression and assert my authority.

Instead of the twenty-five nervous faces I was used to seeing in past years, however, what I saw instead unnerved me and put me totally off stride: To the last one, the students in the classroom were too busy using their thumbs to push tiny keys on the small black objects they held in front of them to even notice me.

CHAPTER 2

I WALKED INTO THE SAME CLASSROOM where I had made my debut as a college professor over twenty years ago. The room had been spruced up a bit since then, with new desks and light fixtures. It had even been painted. As I made my way to the lectern, the students barely acknowledged me. They continued to text or chat among themselves. I busied myself with opening my briefcase to take out copies of the course outline. It crossed my mind that maybe no one used course outlines anymore. Without looking up, I turned to what used to be a blackboard and discovered a shiny whiteboard. I picked up one of several markers and tried to write the number and title of the course and my name; however, it and the next two markers were drier than my mouth was quickly becoming.

Why was I doing this? Why was I putting myself through something I didn't need or want?

As I turned to face the class, the door opened and Randy Webb stepped into the room. After a quick glance of reassurance to me, he put a finger at each corner of his mouth and whistled loudly.

When enough of the students didn't look up, he did it again, even louder. Then he walked to my side and shook my hand.

"Sorry, Tom. I should've been here sooner. I got delayed in dropping my kid off at day care. Karen has a dental appointment today. Let me get these guys warmed up for you."

He turned toward the students, most of whom were now paying attention. "I know you all got new iPhones or Droids or some other device for Christmas, but now is not the time to practice your texting skills. You are giving me and our distinguished instructor a very bad impression. This is not junior high, as many of you will find out when grade time rolls around, and we don't spend our time up here busting our . . ." he paused for dramatic effect and a few students started smirking, "backs to have you sit there and ignore us when we come in here to unload all the knowledge we possess." Webb jabbed his head with a finger. "There is so much in mine that it would take me years to pour it all out."

After playing the proverbial bad cop, he was now playing the good cop. From the many smiles I saw in the audience, the technique seemed to be working.

"Okay, with that out of the way, I want to introduce a man who joined this department when most of you were in grade school or maybe not even alive yet."

He looked out at the students. "Kristy, are you with us? Am I right?"

A pretty girl with long blond hair smiled from the front row, while putting her iPhone in her purse. "Yes sir."

"Samuel?"

A tall, Black kid in the second row with his cap on backwards looked up. "Yo, Mr. Webb."

"You are ready to pay attention, I know you are."

"I am, yes sir."

"You needn't get too carried away with all this 'sir' stuff, but I am making a point here. You need to pay attention. Now, back to your instructor."

I was getting a bit uncomfortable at all the emphasis on me, even though I have my share of ego. Of course, these kids did not know me, so maybe what Webb was doing would be helpful in the long run. In the past, I'd known every student in the room for several years and had them in many classes.

"Before joining this department, Professor Thomas Martindale had a distinguished career as a magazine journalist in New York. After coming to Oregon University, he helped make the department run the way it does now. We try to give you experience so you can learn by doing. We try to keep classes small so you don't get lost in the shuffle like you could at that mighty 'J' school to the south—that big, bad University of you-know-where."

"Boo, Ducks. Yay, Beavers," yelled several students in the back of the room.

"Along the way, Tom continued his investigative reporting and uncovered some pretty nasty stuff at OU. A biologist, a fairly important biologist, was trying to experiment on human subjects to find a cure for a deadly virus. Right here on our bucolic campus, if you can believe it. Then Tom ran afoul of some pretty nasty drug guys from across the border—and I don't mean the California border. He got out of it alive and wrote about it in a book that became a bestseller, *The Cocaine Trail*."

The students were paying close attention now. I was even becoming enthralled by my own story. Was that me he was talking about?

"He is dying—no pun intended—to tell you all about it. He's got more experience as a journalist and writer than the rest of the faculty combined." Webb put his hand up to his mouth. "Don't tell the other faculty members I said that."

The students were smiling and shaking their heads in a knowing way.

"At any rate, the university granted him a leave without pay several years ago so he could write his book. I coaxed him into coming back this term because we are short-handed and the department needs him. You need him. It is my honor to introduce Professor Thomas Martindale."

My face felt hot as it always does when I'm embarrassed. I shook Webb's hand and leaned toward him. "What a build-up. Thanks. Will you do this for every class, every day?"

"You're on your own now, buddy," he whispered. "Good luck. Drop by my office later and let me know how it goes."

Webb walked quickly from the room. The students were now paying attention to me.

"Wow, what a great introduction. I just told Mr. Webb that I expected him to do that every day."

No one even cracked a smile at my lame attempt at humor.

"This is a course in mass media careers. As Mr. Webb said, I've had a long one, but some of the things I've done are now passé. The world of journalism—or that current buzzword 'mass media'—has changed a lot since I got my first job. Newspapers and magazines are struggling. Many have gone out of business. Network news is less important than cable news operations where shouting and innuendo have taken the place of honest reporting. Online publications are thriving. Everybody who thinks they have something profound to say has a blog or a Facebook page.

You can check the news on those devices you were using when I came in—please don't show me how you do it right now. Writing has changed too, and not always for the best. The abbreviations you use to keep in touch with one another when you text are not acceptable when you write professionally. Conventional spelling and proper grammar are still required. That's where old-timers like me come in. I may not have worked in any of these new mass media entities, but I still know how to write. And that's why I came back: to help you stand out as writers and editors. In spite of what you may have heard, being good at the old-fashioned skills of writing and editing will still get you a job and help you keep it, more than knowing how to operate all the gee-whiz gizmos in the world."

I paused for effect. They were paying attention.

"But this is not a course where I will be the only teacher. This is a careers course. I'll lecture once in a while, but mostly I'll be the MC for a group of people who work in different parts of this crazy business. I've asked them to come here to tell you about what they do and to give you some tips on how to get started." I closed my folder. "Any questions?"

The young woman Webb had talked to before raised her hand.

"Kristy, is it?" It was a miracle I had remembered her name, and she seemed pleased that I did.

"Yes, that's right. I want to be a fashion editor at one of those glossy magazines published in New York."

"Sure, I know them well—*Vogue, Harper's Bazaar, Mademoiselle.*"

"Is it foolish to try for them, given all the changes that are going on? I mean, magazines are dying, like you said."

"Those publications will never die as long as women like nice clothes. The competition is tough, but if you're good, they'll make a place for you. Maybe by starting as an intern."

The Black guy put up his hand. I nodded at him.

"Yes sir, Mr. Martingale."

I let the mistake with my name go by.

"Is it a myth that minority people like me have a better chance at getting into the biz than in the bad old days when you started out?"

"I think it is a bit easier . . . Samuel, is it?"

He nodded. Two out of two names right wasn't bad.

"A lot of companies have internship programs for minorities, but you still need to have the ability to function once you get your foot in the door. I'd be happy to help you find one." I glanced at my watch. "We are almost out of time. I'll leave these course outlines—you do still get typed course outlines handed out to you at the beginning of class? I mean, I don't have to send them to you via an email?"

Many of the students smiled or laughed.

"Okay, we've got time for one more question. Yes, you in the back in the corner." I nodded at a young woman who had continued to work her thumbs on the tiny keyboard of some kind of device the whole time I had been talking. When she answered, she spoke in that Valley girl cadence that is so easy to mock.

"All of this old stuff sounds so lame. I have a more important question for you. Ya know, like, I mean, will you, ya know, be talkin' this term about the time you were arrested for murder? I mean, like for killin' that chick you were, like, maybe havin' a, ya know, affair with?"

There were gasps from the class as I felt my face turning red yet again.

CHAPTER 3

"MY GOD, RANDY. Things have gotten pretty frank and brutal on the front lines of the classroom."

I had retreated to Webb's office as soon as I had gathered my material and mumbled something like "see you next class" on my way quickly out of the classroom.

"I'm sorry, Tom. I guess respect toward faculty is not a given anymore. That sounds like Tina Alsop—thin girl dressed to the nines with lots of curls and a lot of makeup?"

"Yeah, and who talks, ya know, like an empty-headed Valley girl."

"Comes from a wealthy Portland family and drives a Mercedes. Her father's an attorney and her mother is from a timber family. What happens these days is that kids have instant access to the world through the Internet on their iPhones or iPads and through Facebook. It was only a matter of time before she or someone else put your name in a search engine just out of curiosity. The arrest was probably noted somewhere and that was that. Not so kind of her to blurt it out, but she's like a lot of other college students today: they have no boundaries. If all that information is out there for the taking, they will grab it and use it. They spend half their lives texting each other about everything. Your old arrest record is no exception."

"Yeah," I sighed. "Of course, it is true. I was arrested briefly, but I got out of jail the next morning. It's just not something I'm ready to talk about in public."

"That's the point these days, Tom. There is no *private*. It's all *public*. You've got to remember how we all love gossip. Hell, a lot of media today feature nothing else. And these kids grew up in that kind of news culture. It's not like what she said is a secret you're trying to keep from me or the dean or the university. My advice would be to embrace this tiny bit of notoriety and let it become part of your mystique."

"You're right, I guess, but this kind of stuff makes me feel very old and out of touch," I said.

"You *are* old, Tom," Webb said with a smile, "but you're not out of touch."

I felt a bit better when I left his office and headed for my own, down the hall. I walked through the door and locked it behind me, then sat down at a table in the small conference room connected to my office and thought about what to do.

Randy was right. My arrest was public knowledge and had been for several years. It just hadn't come up on the radar of these students who were probably in middle school at the time. The best way to diffuse this was to react to it in a nonchalant way and treat it like the old news it was. If it came up again, I'd say something like "What else is new" or "Next question" and then smile.

* * * * *

I brought a tuna sandwich and coffee back to my office and made some notes for my next class while I ate. This one was more to my liking because it was a graduate seminar on book writing.

An hour later, I strolled into the small room two doors down from my office before the students began arriving. I distributed the course outlines in front of six places on the round table and wrote my name and the course name and number on the whiteboard. This time, the marker had plenty of ink.

J-517 Seminar on Book Writing
Thomas Martindale

I glanced at the few notes I had made. When I first started teaching, I was a prisoner of the podium and my written lecture. I found out fairly quickly that I might run out of something to say after twenty minutes . . . with another thirty left. In my first class, I started sweating at that point and was at a loss for what to do next. Pretty soon I discovered that students really didn't like instructors to read from a formal lecture but rather preferred to be talked to in a conversational tone. So I got used to writing down broad topics that I could refer to as I went along. I even left the podium! Sometimes I walked back and forth in front of the front row of desks. Everything became much more relaxed, and the students and I actually had a good time.

My notes for today's class were:
- *Introduce self and tell about background and qualifications to teach this course*
- *Talk about course requirements, deadlines, final projects*
- *Have students introduce selves and talk about their book ideas*

The door opened and two slightly older than average students entered the room. I quickly got up and walked over to them.

"Tom Martindale. Good afternoon. Welcome to the class."

"Kate Knowland."

The woman looked to be in her forties and was as plain as the gossip girl from the other class had been flashy: no makeup, hair pulled back, wearing a nondescript green jacket, crew-neck sweater, and brown cords.

The man held out his hand. "Peter Ogle. I'm a graduate student in the department, and I'm really interested in your help to tell my story."

He was tall and thin and had the look of someone who had not had an easy life. His face was a bit haggard, and he had a shaved head with a long goatee that was gray and a bit unkempt. A menacing tattoo on his neck showed slightly from under his faded sweatshirt. While I probably wouldn't cross the street to get away from Peter, I might consider it.

The two of them sat down at opposite sides of the table and began reading the course outline.

A clean-cut young guy in his thirties came in next. He was dressed in pressed slacks, a button-down shirt, a V-neck wool sweater, and a down vest that probably cost more than what Peter and Kate—and maybe I—had paid for our clothes.

"Ned Tateman."

We shook hands and he sat down next to Ogle, immediately shaking his hand and nodding across the table at Kate.

Next to arrive was a stunning redhead dressed in green—from high-necked wool sweater to tweed pants and high boots. Her makeup had been perfectly applied and her hair carefully coiffed, although I am not much of an expert on either subject. She looked a bit older than the average graduate student, maybe in her early thirties.

"Hello. I'm Amanda Morrison."

"Tom Martindale. Welcome to my class."

I handed her an outline, and she sat down to read it—away from all the other students.

The door opened again and an older woman I thought I had seen before came in. She was dressed like your average aunt: a print dress, sensible shoes, and—despite the fact that it was spring—a wool coat with, of all things, a fur collar.

I smiled and extended my hand. "Tom Martindale."

"You don't remember me, now do you?" she said.

When this happens on the book trail, I always try to take the route of a politician with no aide at his side to brief him in a receiving line by saying "Nice to see you again." Now I would have no such assistance.

"We met at your signing last year at the mystery bookstore in Portland," she said and waited expectantly for my reply.

I had done kind of a trial run at the mystery bookstore before starting on my national tour. The audience had been full of older women, most belonging to a reading group. I remembered that this one had been alone and a bit of a handful—very opinionated and a bit grouchy.

"I know you weren't in the reading group and you came by yourself. It was a cold night, and you had on a heavy coat and a long scarf."

She was beginning to smile, I guess because I remembered her.

"However, your name escapes me. I am sorry, but I've never been very good at names. Faces, yes, but not names."

"Gertrude Snyder." She sat down.

"And you offered to help the Russian guy."

"Yes, I did that and I wanted to . . ."

This whole thing was taking far too long. I glanced at my watch and saw that it was several minutes past the time to begin class. Because they had nothing better to do, the other students had been listening to this whole exchange.

"Hold that thought," I said and patted her arm. "I need to get this class going."

I turned to the others. "We got a bit carried away in our reminiscing. Welcome to J-517, Seminar on Book Writing. There were supposed to be six of you but I guess . . ."

"Oh, I forgot. The secretary in the office asked me to give you this slip." Amanda Morrison handed it across the table to me.

"A drop slip, I'd guess. Well, it will just be the six of us. A real luxury for everyone—we'll have so much more time to talk and go over your work."

To keep a relaxed atmosphere, I always stayed seated in seminars, getting up only when I had to write on the board.

"The outline indicates what I hope we can accomplish this term. After I give you some general background on book publishing today, I will review the nuts and bolts of how a book gets published. Then, we will spend the rest of the term getting your book ready for submission to an agent or a publisher. I presume that you all have book projects."

I looked up. They all nodded.

"Good. I hope they're all nonfiction books. I don't write fiction although the process is the same for both, up to a point."

I looked around at them again. "All nonfiction?" They nodded once again.

"Great. Next, I'd like to go around the table and have you tell me and the rest of the class a bit about yourselves and the book you are planning to write. I'll begin while you collect your thoughts."

I glanced around the table and all five of them were looking at me, no texting or Tweeting in this crowd. This was going to be the kind of class I was used to.

"I grew up in Santa Monica, California, and got two degrees from UCLA. I went to work right out of college for a small, political magazine in New York, then switched to a business magazine, and eventually wound up in the investigative unit at *Newsweek*. After over fifteen years in active journalism, I got tired of the pressure of deadlines and the constant travel and was hired here at Oregon University to teach journalism. I moved to Corvallis about twenty years ago and have been here on and off ever since. For the past few years, I have been on a leave without pay to write several books. I was lucky to have my first book, *The Cocaine Trail,* become a bestseller for a brief time. I am back this term to help out Professor Webb, the department chair, who is short of instructors. That's it."

I looked away from Gertrude because I feared she would take us on an overly long story that might take up all the time we had. I had written their names on a copy of the course outline, and I glanced at the list.

"Kate. Would you start, please?"

"Sure, I can do that. I'm Kate Knowland, and I'm working on a master's degree here in the department. As you can see, I'm a bit older than the regular graduate student because I got married pretty young and had a couple of kids and didn't go to college until they were grown. And, oh yes, my husband left me a couple of years ago for a younger woman."

The others took this all in without any reaction except for Gertrude, who shook her head and got red in the face. "That bastard," she muttered.

Kate went on. "I'd always liked to write and people told me I was good at it, so I decided to see if I had any talent. So with the support of my kids, I came back to school. And here I am. The book I want to write is about rape and the victims of rape. I'll tell my own story and then include material from four other women who were also raped. I know them and will interview them. That's my story. It seems like a good subject for a book."

I was impressed by her ability to discuss something so horrible and personally damaging in such a dispassionate way. I took a swig of water and spoke.

"You've got that right. Very powerful. I applaud you for being willing to share your story with us today and your future readers."

The other students seemed stunned by what they had heard. Ned Tateman broke the silence.

"Not to be trite, but that's a tough act to follow," he said. "What I've got in mind is not all that deep, but I still think it will make a good book."

Ned was one of those people who got people's attention because he was good looking and dressed well.

"I spent two years in the Peace Corps when I graduated from college," he began. "Most of the time I was assigned to a remote area of Peru. There was a lot of valuable work to be done for the impoverished people living there, and they welcomed us. But this was just after the Shining Path rebel group had been brought down by the government and their insurgency ended. A lot of blood had been shed on both sides. The Shining Path had been brutal in the way they terrorized the whole country for years with many bombings and assassinations. The army didn't take many prisoners; they killed almost everyone associated with the rebels and didn't try to sort out who had done what.

"The village I was assigned to was in a remote valley in the foothills of the Andes Mountains. There were five of us on the team; I was assigned to train teachers, while others concentrated on economic matters—like starting a system to market woven goods and setting up a water purification system."

Ned paused and took a drink of water. I looked at the other students and saw that they were paying close attention. I was very pleased: two good book ideas and a class of interesting people. This kind of situation is what teachers wish for but do not always find. Who decides to take a course in a particular term will make or break that course. Sometimes you dread the final day of the term because the magic of the class will be shattered. Other times, you can't wait for the misery to end. With this group, I already knew I'd be missing the magic in ten weeks.

"After a few days, I saw the people in the village coming and going out of a small house on the edge of the jungle. It was built better than the other buildings and looked larger from the outside. When they walked to the house, the villagers were usually carrying food or parcels wrapped in newspaper.

"As a guest in the village, I had decided early on to keep my curiosity in check. I worried that if I asked too many probing questions, they would quit trusting me and that would interfere with my work. If people wanted me to know the story of who lived in the building, they would tell me. And my colleagues on the team seemed too busy to care about what went on inside that house.

"Two weeks passed and one day after school, I walked outside and was amazed to see a tiny woman sitting on the front porch of the house. Her eyes were closed, and she appeared to be soaking up the sun as she rocked back and forth in her chair. A large man with a mustache and a fierce look on his face stood behind her chair, his eyes following me as I turned to walk back toward the compound where we lived.

" 'Señor,' a faint voice said behind me, 'would you help an old lady improve her English?' I turned and started walking back to where she was sitting. The big guy glared and stepped in front of her, his hand in the pocket of his loose-fitting coat. 'Manuel, bastante!' She put her frail arm up to stop him from walking any closer to me. I ignored him and walked to her. 'Señora, it is a pleasure to meet you.' I bowed and took her hand, which I kissed gently. She smiled. 'I seldom encounter a true gentleman in the jungle.' "

Ned stopped talking and looked at the others at the table. "Are you hooked?" He broke into a big smile.

"Don't stop!" someone said.

"Keep going," said someone else.

"You're all going to hate me, I know, but we are out of time," I said. "When we come back on Thursday, we'll try to coax Ned into finishing his story. And Ned, don't give anyone the punch line of your story until then. Okay?"

"You bet. I promise."

The other students filed out except for Ned and Gertrude. She walked to where I was sitting and sat down beside me. Why did it not surprise me that she would probably always need extra attention? Older students are that way. They might bring a lot of life experience into the discussion, but they can also be a pain in the neck because they think that their agenda is more important than anyone else's.

"Stick around, Ned, if you can," I said. He nodded and sat down across the table.

"So, Gertrude, I was surprised to see you here. I thought you lived in Portland. Are you a full-time student?"

"No, I'm still living in Portland," she said. "But I've got a grandson going to school here, and he talked me into taking your course and another one on English poetry. I'm not going for a degree, of course. I got one years ago in La Grande. I got inspired by your talk in the bookstore and then I helped that Russian man with his book and helped some other people in my writing group get started with their stories. So I guess I just wanted some time at the feet of the master—you!"

Of course, I felt my face turn red on cue. All of this adoration was making me nervous. I glanced at Ned. He was pretending to read a book but covering his face to hide his smile.

"I am so honored that I had such an impact on you, Gertrude." I stood up. "I'll do my best to help you with your writing."

"But I wanted to talk to you about my book. It's about . . ."

I put up my hand.

"I can't let you tell me," I said. "It wouldn't be fair to the others. I'll just have to wait until next class. Okay?"

Gertrude sighed and stood up, gathering up the papers she had already scattered around on the table in front of me.

"I guess you know best. All right. I'll wait. But can't I even tell you the subject?"

"No, no," I sighed. "As I said, it wouldn't be fair to the others."

* * * * *

"You really had an impact on Mrs. Snyder," said Ned a bit later in my office. I had stopped off in the coffee room and poured cups for the two of us. I was now sitting behind my desk, and he was in the chair opposite me.

"I love older students," I said. "But they can get carried away with themselves and what they want to write about. Sometimes their topics are interesting but often they are pretty boring to anyone but a family member. Gertrude won't ever be a professional writer, and my task this term will be to get her to realize that and just do a good job of turning her idea into a book she can have published for her family. Even without hearing about it, I'd be willing to bet that it is about growing up on a ranch in eastern Oregon or attending a one-room school over there or something similar."

Ned nodded. "The reason I hung around is to ask you if you might know my mother. She went to high school in Santa Monica, maybe at the time you were there."

"What's her name?"

"Margot Tateman. Her maiden name was Duncan."

"My God, I did know her. We weren't close friends, but we were in student government together. How is she?"

"She's fine. She came up here for college and met my dad. His name is Michael—Mike. He's an attorney in Portland. I have one sister who is married to an attorney, and they live in Seattle with two kids. I've been a bit of a slow starter. I did two tours in the Peace Corps and kind of bummed around Europe for a couple of years. I did get a degree from Reed College but was a bit of a screw-up working as a coffee *barista* and a waiter for a couple of years. That's why I'm a bit older than some of the students in the department. I'm thirty."

"Wow, Margot's son. I can't get over the small-world aspect of this. Please give your mom my best. Tell her I'll take good care of you in my class."

"Knowing her, she'll want to have you for dinner so you can meet my dad. She's quite the hostess."

"I'd really like that," I said.

CHAPTER 4

NOTES FROM THE CLASS FROM HELL

"We'll have our first guest speaker next week," I said in a louder than usual voice in order to be heard above the din of the clicking keys of the students' iPhones. I wished that Randy was here to blast them with one of his whistles.

"GOOD MORNING, GANG. REMEMBER ME? I'M THE GUY WHO GOT SPRUNG FROM JAIL SO I COULD BE YOUR TEACHER!"

That got their attention. In fact, it got so quiet you could hear the proverbial pin drop.

"Great, something worked to bring you back to this world. You know, I could whine about your inattention, but I don't think that would work, do you? Let's just say that I strongly recommend that you either quit texting when you come in this room or make the choice to not come back to this room and drop the class. Now, I have arranged for some people to talk to you each week about their jobs in the publishing industry. You might even

learn something. If you'd rather text or Tweet about last night's date or who is having sex with whom, far be it for me to stop you. Just don't do it in here or I will, literally, boot you out."

Smirks all around. Tina, the girl who had asked the embarrassing question about my past raised her hand.

"What. Ever. I mean about that arrest. Did you really kill that woman and, if you did, how did you get out of jail?"

* * * * *

"Good afternoon. Hope you had a good weekend. If there aren't any questions, we'll go back to your book ideas. Ned was about to tell us more about the old lady in the jungle." I nodded to him.

"Yes, I was about to do just that. So, I walked closer to her so I could hear her—her voice was really tiny and faint. Over the next hour or so, she told me the story about how she had been the only doctor for the insurgents living in the jungle. There were a lot of them living in the cities of Peru too. She was born in Bolivia but trained in Cuba, which has a very good medical education system, and got an MD degree when she was in her late fifties. Although she looked frail, she was tough enough to endure the rigors of jungle life and the stress from being on the run from government troops for years. She was never charged with anything: I guess the government did not arrest her because of her age, and now she was retired. I spent a lot of time with her over the next year of my posting in the area and took a lot of notes. At the time, I wasn't sure what I would do with the material. Now, I know. I want to write a book about her. Her name, by the way, is Dolores Figueroa. She's still living in the town where I last saw her. I had a message from her last month. I guess that's it."

"Young man," said Gertrude Snyder, "I think you have the makings of a good book there. I know I'd read it, and I usually read only mysteries and true crime books, like the one written by our professor."

"This is a good story, Ned," I said. "Some subjects are better covered in magazine articles and doing them as a book means you have to put in a lot of padding, but I think it would take a book to do your story justice. You could weave *Señora* Figueroa's story in with the broader subject of what that long-time insurgency did to Peru and how stamping it out did some permanent damage to the country's civil liberties."

After a moment, I looked around the table and said, "Who's next?"

Peter Ogle cleared his throat, shuffled some pages, and said, "I'll go. What I'm going to tell you about is not easy to put into words in front of strangers. It has made me an alcoholic and a drug addict. I've been in therapy. I've been in alcohol treatment programs. And I still can't forget what happened to me."

The others shifted uneasily in their chairs, their eyes glued to him.

"I'm a vet, as you can probably tell by the way I dress and the way I look. I mean, these tats"—he pointed to his neck—"you don't get them if you're in a white collar job or a profession. You get them during a drunken night on the town when you're trying to forget stuff you've done—bad stuff that you had to do while following orders."

He picked up the pages and straightened them by tapping them on the table.

"My specialty in the army was to operate a flamethrower. The concept had been around for centuries, but it was used extensively in World War II and Vietnam. You've seen them in documentaries about war or action movies with lots of bad guys. In reality, it is a death machine, especially if it is aimed at people. We normally incinerated military vehicles with it, however. The M2A1-7 model I used was not all that different from earlier versions. It was designed to project a long and controlled stream of fire.

"Vehicles were my target during the first Gulf War, Operation Desert Storm—the so-called *good* war with Iraq. The Iraqis had invaded Kuwait, and we got them out of there in a few days. When they retreated into their country, most of them used the one main highway running north. What may have been orderly at first turned into a chaotic run-for-your-life situation fairly quickly. It also turned into a highway of death. In fact, I think that is what the books about the war call it today.

"On the second day of this retreat, my unit was ordered to drive up the highway and obliterate the vehicles both on the highway and for a half-mile on either side of it. We needed to clear the way for our own vehicles. To make a long story short, we did just that—and with a vengeance. Like kids with matches, we set fire to tanks and trucks and even cars. I mean, the highway was littered with late-model Cadillacs and Mercedes the Iraqi army had stolen from the Kuwaitis.

"Our unit was commanded—if you can call it that—by a shave-tail second lieutenant who did not know his—forgive me ladies—ass from a hole in the ground. On the second day, we came upon one of these big cars. I can't remember what kind. It was crammed with people and had a bunch of stuff tied onto the roof. A big man with a big mustache—all Iraqi men have big mustaches, I suppose so they looked like Saddam Hussein—was driving. He had on a uniform and even a helmet. As our Humvee came up on the back of this car, I could see that it was full of women and children: some Iraqi officer was rushing back to his country and taking his family with him. Maybe they'd been allowed to live with him, maybe they had lived in Kuwait. Whatever. This was not a military vehicle by any means, so I put my flamethrower down.

"The lieutenant, I think his name was Hastings, started shouting at me. He had been riding the crew for weeks. He had no knowledge of what we did or the rules we were trained to follow in doing what we did. He was one of those officers who let the insignia on his uniform go to his head. And he pulled rank on us for everything. I mean, in all the filthy conditions we had been enduring for weeks, he still made us shave and, if you can believe it, polish our boots. That requirement was finally ended by his superior officer for being too excessive in wartime."

Then Peter raised his voice.

" 'KILL THOSE FUCKERS,' the lieutenant started shouting. 'YOU'RE LETTING THEM GET AWAY!'

" 'SIR, THEY'RE CIVILIANS! WE SHOULD GET THEM TO STOP AND AT LEAST TALK TO THEM!'

"At that point, the lieutenant grabbed the flamethrower from me and pointed it at the car. We had picked up speed and were looming over it; in fact, we were practically touching the rear bumper. The lieutenant pulled the firing trigger and a huge tongue of flame hit the car. I tried to grab the flamethrower from him, but he pulled back to keep it away from me. As he did, he lost his balance and fell into the flame himself. I watched his head burst into flame and, at the same time, heard screams from the people in the car ahead. The car slowed and came to a stop; the driver of our vehicle did the same. With the smell of burning flesh all around me, I jumped down from our vehicle to see if I could help anyone.

Eight people—the man, his wife, an older woman, and five chil-dren—were in the car, all burned beyond recognition."

All three women in the room were crying, and both Ned and I were on the verge. No wonder Ogle looked like he did. His past had done more than haunt him—it had nearly consumed him.

"Well, I didn't mean to upset everybody," he said softly. "But that is the God's truth about what happened. I think that's enough of my story for right now."

This kind of thing had happened once or twice in my career as a university professor—where a student uses writing as a catharsis. It is always in an upper division or graduate class. Freshmen and sophomores have either not had much happen to them or they were incapable of expressing it. They were too busy with their dating and sex and gossiping that I suppose they were always texting about.

"Peter," I said in a hoarse voice that I tried to improve by clear-ing my throat a couple of times, "that is a powerful story. I'm glad you felt comfortable enough to tell us. I think we need to wind up for today. We've got two ideas to go—from Gertrude and Amanda. We'll hear them next time."

The students filed out with somber looks on their faces. Gertrude Snyder was still dabbing at her eyes with a handker-chief. Only Ned Tateman stayed behind.

"I thought I'd seen a lot of bad stuff," he said, shaking his head. "Nothing as bad as that, though. Really powerful story."

"I agree. I hope Peter is up to reliving it as he writes about it. I admire the way he told it all to us. That took courage."

"Yeah, we are all strangers with our writing being the only common element," said Ned. "I think it's neat that it's bringing us together."

"Sometimes it is easier to tell bad things to people you don't know because they concentrate on the story, not any baggage you might have," I said.

Ned stood up, gathered his papers, and put them in a backpack.

"I wanted to tell you that my mom was really excited when I told her that I'd met you. As I predicted, she wants to have you over for dinner to catch up and have you meet my dad. I'm not sure how soon it will be because he travels a lot. He's a rainmaker in the firm. Do you know what that is?"

"He is well connected and brings in new clients, preferably ones with a lot of money," I laughed.

"You got *that* right. He's been doing this for so long that corporate law bores him, so he tries to do as much pro bono work as he can—ACLU stuff, child advocacy cases, that kind of thing. He also does a lot of mediation."

"That is really admirable," I said. "I'll look forward to meeting him and, of course, seeing your mom again."

CHAPTER 5

GIVEN THE WEEK I HAD HAD, I decided to treat myself to a weekend in Portland. I had never lived in Oregon's largest city, but I loved going there because of all the cultural things to do there—new movies, plays, concerts, art galleries. I liked living on the coast and, on rare occasions like now, the college town of Corvallis, but there is no substitute for a metropolitan area.

I left my rented condo on Saturday morning and drove up Interstate 5 to the big city. I had made reservations at a downtown hotel. I settled into my room and decided to check my phone messages before I went out to have lunch and see a movie.

"You have one new message," said the friendly voicemail message, which then gave me the message.

"Tom, hi, it's Margot Tateman, or should I say Margot Duncan? Ned told me that he was taking a class from you. Small world, don't you think? I was calling to see if we could arrange to get together. I'd love to have you here for dinner to chat, and I want you to meet my husband, Mike. Please call me so we can set something up."

I jotted down her number and decided, on a whim, to call her right then before I left the room. The phone rang three times.

"Hello."

"Margot Duncan?"

There was a pause.

"Yes."

"This is a voice from your past."

"Tom. So good to hear from you. I guess you got my message. But I only called you two hours ago."

"I'm a fast worker," I said laughing. "Good to hear your voice too."

"We've got so much to catch up on."

"Like thirty-five years worth."

"When can you come up for lunch or dinner? I'd love for you to meet Mike, as I said in my message."

"That's why I was calling. I'm in Portland right now. I needed to get away for the weekend and drove here. Once I checked in, I called for my messages and got yours. And here I am."

"Gosh, that is terrific. But Mike is in New York attending a conference." She paused for a moment or two. "Why don't you come over anyway. We can get all of our reminiscing out of the way and then you can meet him another time. I'll throw something together. How about 7 o'clock?"

"I'd love it."

I wrote down her address and the directions to her house.

"I'll see you then."

* * * * *

The Tatemans lived in a condo development on the east side of the Willamette River. I drove up to the gate and punched in the code she had given me.

"Hello."

"Margot, it's Tom."

"Okay, stand by to drive in when the gate opens."

The tall, iron gate came creakily to life and slid to the right. I drove in and turned to the right and parked in one of the spaces reserved for visitors. I walked through the front door of the building and into the elevator. The Tatemans lived on the second floor. The door opened into a private entry hall. I turned to the right and walked to the door marked 2-A. Before I could punch the bell, the door opened and Margot was standing there.

"Tom. I'm so glad to see you." She stepped back and looked at me as if framing a subject for a photograph. "I'd recognize you anywhere. You've still got that wonderful smile."

"You've still got all that dark, curly hair," I replied.

"With lots of gray in it."

She had not changed all that much. She had been a cheerleader in high school and a member of the prize-winning drill team that performed at football games. While dressing and acting more sedately now, she still retained the vibrancy she had then. And she was just as pretty, even with a few lines here and there in her face.

"Come in. Let me take your coat."

I took off my coat and handed it to her.

"We'll go in here." She motioned me down a hall and into a living room with large windows that looked out on a deck and the river beyond.

"This is a wonderful place," I said. "I wouldn't get any work done here. I'd be gazing constantly at the river."

I walked to the door and opened it, stepping out onto the deck. Even though it had been a sunny day, it was a bit cold because of a wind coming off the river, which lay a few hundred yards below.

"Kind of cold for spring," she said from behind me. "You'll have to come back in the summer. That is a glorious place to sit."

I walked back into the living room.

"Red or white?" She motioned to wine bottles sitting on a counter at the other end of the room.

"White would be great."

She poured two glasses and sat down opposite me in a chair in front of the fireplace.

"To reunions."

"I'll definitely drink to that," I said, raising my glass. "So, how long have you lived here?"

"Ten years. We wanted a smaller place after the kids moved out. We used to have a house in the West Hills." She gestured toward the river and the higher elevation beyond. The West Hills was one of Portland's most exclusive areas. "Ned says you live on the coast. Where exactly?"

"North of Newport, in an area that is south of the Yaquina Head Lighthouse."

"I know that area well. We have often taken the kids to the lighthouse and we once attended a political reception at the home of the senator who used to live near there." She took another sip of wine.

"So, give me a synopsis of the last thirty-five years," I said.

For the next four hours we did just that, taking turns recounting what we had done since high school, between bites of a delicious dinner. I loved doing this and Margot seemed to share that sentiment. She told me about raising her two kids and her life as a high school art teacher and then as an interior decorator. I told

her about my career as a journalist and as a university professor.
I did not go into my scrape with the law but did tell her a little bit
about my amateur sleuthing, the run-in with the drug gang, and
my best-selling book about that unnerving experience.

Then I looked at my watch and was surprised to see that it
was 11 o'clock. "I've got to get going. I don't want to overstay my
welcome," I said, getting up from the table.

"The time really flew," she said, carrying some of the dishes
into the kitchen. I followed her with more of them.

We walked to the front door, and she got my coat from the
closet. I put it on and hugged her.

"It has been wonderful to see you again, Margot. There's nothing like old friends to soothe one's soul."

She frowned.

"I'm sorry if your soul needs soothing," she said, cocking
her head sympathetically. "Come anytime you want to bare your
soul—or soothe it."

I stepped through the door and turned back to face her. "All of
this talk about my soul is making me very nervous," I said, smiling. "I've known people who doubt I have one."

"Poor Tom. Always a loner. Tell Aunt Margot all your troubles
next time."

All of my difficulties with women flooded into my head:
Maxine March and Angela Pride before her.

"You don't know the half of it. Maybe next time."

Astute women often have the ability to read minds, I have
found, or at least to sense things that may be too personal to talk
about. Although my underlying sadness was not really the result
of bad relationships, I often wondered why I could not keep a

girlfriend for very long. Maybe Margot could give me her secret of stability.

"I'll say goodnight and hope to see you again soon and meet Mike." I bowed and kissed her hand.

"Why, Tom," she said and smiled. "I did not remember you as being so chivalrous."

CHAPTER 6

NOTES FROM THE CLASS FROM HELL

"I wanted to talk a bit this morning about my views of the stridency of news on cable TV, particularly the right-leaning Fox News," I said to the texting masses in front of me. "Walter Lippmann was a renowned journalist and political philosopher of the early 20th century, and he once said, 'Man responds as powerfully to fiction as they do to realities [and], in many cases, they help to create the very fictions to which they respond.' Who wants to tell me how that statement applies to cable TV news stations?"

One student looked up. "Say what?" he asked.

Another murmured, "What. Ever."

* * * * *

My other class, the one I considered my "real" class, was going well. Gertrude Snyder and Amanda Morrison presented their proposals. As I had predicted, Gertrude's was an account of her grandmother's career as the teacher in a one-room school in eastern Oregon in the 1880s. Amanda's was more interesting and more saleable. She wrote of her years as a contestant in beauty contests. "It was the JonBenét Ramsey syndrome," she told us. "My mother pushed me into it from the age of six, and I hated every minute of it. We were little girls dressed up and painted up so we looked like hookers." She proposed to call her book "Little Hookers."

When the two of them were finished, I reviewed the schedule for the rest of the term and ended the class.

CHAPTER 7

NOTES FROM THE CLASS FROM HELL

"Before I introduce our guest speaker, Gregory Walsh, editor of one of the biggest weekly newspapers in the Portland area, I want to ask a question. How many of you get your news from newspapers?"

Not one hand went up. Walsh looked disappointed.

"TV—network or cable?"

Again, not a hand in the air.

"So where?"

Most of them mumbled "phone."

That puzzled me. "You get your news over the telephone?" I glanced at Walsh. He gave me a "see what I'm up against" look.

"Duh," said Tina, the girl who talked like she had rocks in her mouth. "What. Ever. We've all got smart phones. I mean, ya know, iPhones or Blackberries or Droids. These have all got apps you can install to get instant access to CNN or Fox or Comedy Central."

I couldn't believe my ears. "You consider Comedy Central a news source?"

"Why not? Jon Stewart's as tuned in as any of those stiffs on Fox or CNN. I also consult YouTube and the Facebook pages of my friends."

"But none of those people have had any training in journalism."

"What. Ever."

* * * * *

"I want to spend some time talking about the history of book publishing and the business of book publishing today," I said later in the day at my "real class." Thank God I had it. "Book publishing is changing every day to the extent that what I tell you this term may be obsolete in a week.

"Right now, there are seven major companies, and several of them are owned by German companies, which control book publishing in the United States. Many of them have what are called imprints within the larger corporation. For example, Scribner, which was the publisher of great writers like Ernest Hemingway and F. Scott Fitzgerald, is now owned by Simon & Schuster.

"Next, let's consider self-publishing, which is becoming more acceptable than it was even a few years ago. There were something like 400,000 books published by their authors last year, versus 200,000 by regular publishers. A self-published book no longer has the stigma it once had. Readers don't care who the publisher is. If they read the blurb on the jacket and like the cover, they'll buy the book. Book marketing is another subject entirely. I'll talk about it later in the term.

"I'll start today by giving you the information you will need to write the book proposals for this course so you can get started on them right away."

I talked about writing a proposal that summed up their book ideas and how they planned to use them in a book. I discussed writing an outline for each chapter, including one-line summaries of what was to be covered. I also discussed the cover letter that goes with the proposal and outline.

"When you've written these items, you will read them in class, I will go over them, and then you can revise them, if necessary. Then I want you to start writing chapters. I'm assuming that you can do this without much additional research, since you all have subjects you are committed to."

I paused and looked around the table. "Am I right?" They all nodded.

"At the end of the term, I will send all of your proposals to my agent, who has promised to critique them. I have asked her to look at them to see if they have any hope of attracting the attention of a publisher."

All of the students were smiling at that bit of news, except Gertrude.

"I don't think mine would ever be that good," she said.

She was probably right, but I couldn't say so. "You'll be fine. I'll be helping you, and so will your fellow students."

"You will? Thanks so much."

She seemed relieved, especially when Amanda and Kate seconded the offer to help.

"Let me say something about agents at this point," I said. "I am very lucky to have one—and a good one. It is so much easier to attract the attention of a publisher if the manuscript comes to him or her via an agent. However, you can contact publishers directly, and I have done that. I don't believe the stories—spread by agents, no doubt—that you can't even get a publisher to look at a proposal if it comes in directly, without an agent. Agents talk about whole rooms in New York publishing houses that are stacked to the ceilings with unsolicited—and unread—manuscripts. I don't believe that. It just takes longer if it comes in that way, rather than through an agent. The proposals you will be writing will be aimed at working with an agent, but they will also be useful if sent to a publisher directly."

They were all taking notes the old-fashioned way except for Ned, who was using a laptop computer to record what I said. Not a texter in sight!

"I have to be out of town this Thursday, so we will meet again a week from today. I want you to get started on your book proposals and outlines, and we will go over them in class. Any questions?"

No one said a word, including Gertrude.

"Great. Good luck and good writing."

They strolled out of the room, Amanda and Kate walking on either side of Gertrude as if to support her, both in her difficulty of walking and her fear of doing the book proposal. People are good, I thought to myself.

"I hear you and my mom had a good visit," said Ned. "Sorry you didn't get to meet my dad, though. You'd like each other. It seems like he's always traveling, either for business or for pleasure. He's quite the outdoorsman, you know. Loves to explore the rural side of Oregon. My mom hates that kind of thing, and neither my sister nor I like it much either. So he goes alone."

"Good luck to you, Ned. Seems like you know exactly how you want to proceed with your book."

"Yeah. How did you guess?" he smiled and then walked out the door.

Peter Ogle had hung back as the others left, I presumed so he could talk to me alone. In all my years of teaching, I've found these brief encounters to reveal a lot about the people in a class.

"Are you in a hurry, Professor Martindale?" he asked. "Wouldn't want to keep you, if you are."

"No, not at all. Sit down. I hope the course is working for you."

"Oh, yeah, in more ways than you could know. It's just what I needed to get a lot of stuff off my chest. I've been in therapy for years—you know, like at the VA—but it never quite chases away the demons. Mostly those people are not all that helpful, but I had a new therapist a few months ago—a fairly young gal who has since been transferred, wouldn't you know. Anyway, she suggested that I write down what happened to me. Not like as notes but really do a book about it. So I decided to do that and here I am."

"That's good to hear. I did kind of the same thing a year or so ago."

"You suffered from PTSD?" He looked surprised. "Were you in Nam?"

"No. And I wasn't actually diagnosed with PTSD. I did a kind of self-diagnosis. It was after my run-in with the drug gang. I spent a year looking over my shoulder for someone who might be trying to kill me. I finally had enough of it, and that's why I wrote the book."

"I do plan to buy your book."

I held up both hands in front of my face. "Sorry. I'm not trying to sell you a copy. I'm just saying that I know a bit about what you're going through. But, more importantly, I wanted to say that writing the book really helped me get rid of most of the demons that were haunting me."

He nodded. "I stayed behind just to say that going over my story really helped me. It was a lot harder than I thought, but it felt great when I was doing it. A real catharsis, I guess you'd call it. I've never felt better about anything before. This book is really going to help me. I wanted to thank you for making it possible." He reached out and shook my hand. There were tears in his eyes.

"My pleasure," I said, "although I think you are giving me way too much credit."

"Gotta go. I just wanted you to know that I've never looked forward to a class before. See you next week."

Ogle walked quickly out of the room. I gathered up my notes and erased the board. This class was making my return to the university worth it.

CHAPTER 8

THE TIDE WAS OUT THE NEXT MORNING as I walked along the water's edge on the beach below my house near Newport. I had driven over from Corvallis the night before to get away from campus. Because of my part-time status, I was not involved in many departmental activities, but I was still expected to advise some of the graduate students and serve on several committees.

The morning chill caused me to pull up the hood on my sweatshirt. I walked north along the sand toward the Yaquina Head Lighthouse. Since the tide was out, the waves that came in were so small they barely made a sound, almost like along the edge of a lake. The sand was firmly packed so that my shoes barely made indentations as I moved along. I stopped to pick up stones and tiny pieces of wood here and there, many of them shaped like whales. I put them in my pocket as good luck talismans. I had hundreds of them in various glass containers in my study and always carried one in my pocket.

The beach disappeared several hundred yards before I reached the tide pools on the south side of the lighthouse grounds. Anyone wanting to get to these interesting marine hollows had to walk around to the main entrance to the Yaquina Head Lighthouse grounds.

Sea gulls were circling in the sky above me as I turned and headed back down the beach. I could hear the barking of seals in the distance. They loved to loll around on the large rocks slightly off shore.

As I walked, I took deep breaths of the wonderful air. No polluted atmosphere out here, only the occasional smell that was one part seaweed and the other salt.

I spent the rest of the day by myself, reading and working on my two courses—contacting the two remaining guest speakers for the careers class and preparing one more lecture for the book publishing seminar.

I slept late the next morning. After I started the coffee maker and put on a pan of water for oatmeal, I stepped outside to pick up the copy of the *Sunday Oregonian* I had asked a friend to drop off on his way home from church.

The headline for a story on the front page of the Metro section caught my eye as I took the first bite of oatmeal.

PORTLAND ATTORNEY FEARED LOST ON STEENS MOUNTAIN

CHAPTER 9

I RESISTED THE URGE TO CALL MARGOT after I returned to Corvallis. She would have a lot on her mind, and a call from me would be a distraction. Ned was not in class the next day, but the other students wanted to talk about the disappearance of his father. As sometimes happens with small classes, we seemed to have bonded as a group. One of their brethren was in trouble, and they wanted to express their support for him.

"He is such a nice young man," said Gertrude. "I hate to think of him growing up without a father."

"He is in his thirties," said Kate Knowland, not unkindly. "He's not exactly a kid anymore."

Gertrude blew her nose. "I know, I know, but it makes me think of when I lost my father. It was in . . ."

Thankfully, Peter cut her off. "Yeah, losing a dad or a mom is tough at any age. I never knew my dad after about age ten and my mother was a drunk, but I still felt bad when I heard they had died."

"Oh, you poor man." Gertrude's sobbing was now aimed at Peter.

Amanda put her hand on the older lady's shoulder. "Maybe they'll find him, and he'll be okay."

"I hope so, I really do," continued Gertrude, dabbing at her eyes. "Have you talked to Ned?"

"No, I haven't. I really don't know how to reach him here in town. His family lives in Portland, and I assume he's gone up there. If I hear anything, I'll let you all know. Or you'll see it on the news."

Class went on that day in a desultory way, and I was glad when it ended. Two weeks later, the students were still distracted by what had happened to Ned. So was I, but I was still resisting a call to him.

* * * * *

NOTES FROM THE CLASS FROM HELL

"I am pleased to present our next guest speaker, Chad Collins, news director of KWAM, the all news station in Eugene. He will talk about careers in radio. Mr. Collins."

Collins, who looked younger than some of the students, had not bothered to wear a dress shirt or tie or jacket to class. He wore jeans and a sweatshirt, the better to blend in, I suppose. He kept texting up to the time I introduced him.

"Sorry," he mumbled, as he stepped up to the lectern. "A little crisis in the news room. There's been a bomb threat at the federal courthouse in Portland."

"Hi, you guys," he said to the class. A few heads turned to look at him, but many of the students ignored him, as they had ignored the speakers most weeks.

"OKAY, THAT'S IT!" I shouted. "iPHONES OR BLACKBERRIES OR WHATEVER YOU'VE GOT, PUT THEM AWAY OR I'M GOING TO PICK THEM UP! I'VE HAD IT WITH ALL OF YOU!"

Most of the students put down their devices and sat upright in their seats. Except, of course, for Tina Alsop, the girl from the wealthy family who felt that rules were not designed for her to follow. She ignored me and the others and seemed to be listening to music through tiny buttons in both ears. She was so intent on her tunes, and with both eyes closed to better get in the groove of whatever she was listening to, that she did not realize I was standing over her and most of the students had turned in their chairs to face her.

I felt like yanking the ear buds out but decided that might constitute some kind of physical abuse or harassment. Instead, I tapped her on the shoulder. Her eyes opened and she was not the least bit embarrassed.

"I am conducting a class which you seem not to be the least bit interested in," I said through clenched teeth. I picked up her backpack from the floor next to her desk and handed it to her. She stood up and I helped her on with her coat. "I would like you to leave and not come back until you feel you can concentrate on the subject matter."

She smiled as she walked to the door. "What. Ever."

* * * * *

On the way back to my office, I told Randy Webb what I had done and warned him that he might get a call from Tina Alsop's parents. He thanked me but did not seem overly alarmed.

"Her parents travel a lot, and she deals mostly with their assistants."

"As in, 'your people call my people'?"

"I'm afraid so," he said, shaking his head. "No one's ever taught her how to get along in the real world. Her parents just throw money at her. I doubt they really care that much about her. She's a latch key kid, except the key is probably made of gold."

I checked my messages after I closed the door of my office.

"You have one new message. First new message, received today at 10:40 a.m.—Professor Martindale, it's Ned Tateman. My mother wondered if you could come to see us in Portland sometime in the next few days."

CHAPTER 10

"MARGOT, IT'S TOM."

I was waiting in my car outside the gate of Margot's condo building in Portland. When we had talked the day before, we had agreed that I would come up the next day. All kinds of thoughts were turning over in my head during the drive up the freeway. Why had she called me at this particularly difficult time? We were old friends, but we hadn't seen each other for thirty-five years. Our dinner a month ago had been pleasant but hardly a bonding experience.

We were not the same people we had been those many years ago. Even then, we had traveled in different circles. I lived on the less affluent side of town than she. We saw each other mostly in student government activities. We were always friendly enough but had not been close by any means. She didn't know me very well then or now, and I felt the same way about her. Hell, I knew her son Ned better than she did, given all he had shared about his life in the Peace Corps in class.

"Professor Martindale. It's Ned. I'll buzz you in."

The gate came to life and clattered to the right. I was relieved that Ned was here. It was only right that a family member be by her side at a horrible time like this.

He was composed as he opened the door, although his eyes were red. He stepped aside to allow me to enter.

"Mom is in the living room, through here as you probably recall."

Margot was sitting in a chair, waiting for me.

"Don't get up, please," I said. I knelt down and hugged her and patted her on the shoulder. It surprised me that she seemed so composed. I sat down and so did Ned. He cleared his throat.

"Mom, maybe you should tell Professor Martindale why you called him up here. He's got to be pretty curious."

I nodded. "Well, yeah, I guess I am. I'm not sure what I can do for you. I presume you've called the authorities, and they've launched a search of the whole area."

"That's just it," she said. "Somehow, I don't feel like they're putting as much effort as they should into finding Mike. That's why I want you to help us."

Given my perception of Margot's state of mind, I decided I wouldn't try to dissuade her of that notion, at least not at this point. In all of the messes I've gotten into over the past few years, the law enforcement people who have helped me have always wound up nearly apoplectic because of the chances I take to get to the bottom of whatever dilemma I decide to figure out. I'd play along now, with the idea of stepping back as soon as I was certain that Margot was happy with the investigation.

At this point, my old reporter habits kicked in, and I pulled out a pad and pen so I could take notes. If she wanted me to help, I needed to write down some basic facts.

"First, tell me where this happened and when."

She took a sip of water from a glass on the coffee table in front of her. "Mike loves the outdoors and loves nothing more than hiking and camping in the wilderness," she began. "I have to admit that I really don't enjoy roughing it. My idea of camping is to sleep in a tent with real rugs on the floor and a bed to sleep in. No dirty ground or sleeping bag for me."

"You got THAT right," said Ned.

"When we had dinner, I told you that he was on a business trip to New York," she continued. "When he got back, he decided to take a few days off and hike in the desert in southeast Oregon."

"You ever heard of Steens Mountain and the Alvord Desert?" asked Ned.

I nodded. "Heard of them both, but I've never been there."

"Pretty spectacular, but pretty remote," he continued.

"That's what would appeal to Mike," added Margot. "His job could be terribly stressful at times, so he took any opportunity to get away by himself. I'm sure he was secretly glad that I didn't want to go with him on these outings. He needed that time alone to clear his head. I know that sounds corny, but that's the way he was—is. I think he would have chosen a career that would have let him work outdoors, but his father pushed him to go to law school, and he did well." She paused and looked at both Ned and me. "Now, I wish I'd gone with him."

"That's understandable, but you can't blame yourself," I said.

She nodded and resumed her story. "Mike left here two weeks ago for Frenchglen, the tiny town at the entrance to the Steens. He loved to stay in the hotel there. It's really old and doesn't even have bathrooms in every room. Guests all eat together in the dining room, which is also the lobby. He arrived there, checked in, and left early the next morning to walk up the mountain."

"Is the mountain right there?" I asked.

"A couple of miles away, but my dad was a hiker," said Ned. "He was in great condition."

"So he left there and, presumably, walked to the base of the mountain and vanished," said Margot. "No one has seen him since."

"This mountain, is it steep? Do you need mountain climbing gear to scale it?" I asked.

"No need," said Ned. "It's a gradual incline, and you just drive or walk up a gravel road to the top—a bit over 9,000 feet."

"I take it that he didn't come back to the hotel?"

"He did after the first day there," said Ned.

"How do you know all of this?" I asked. "I mean, that he got to the hotel and checked in and went out for a day and came back?"

"We went there as soon as we got the first call from the local sheriff," Margot continued. "We talked to him and the manager of the hotel. The building is owned by the Oregon State Parks Department, but it's operated under a lease arrangement. The guy we talked to runs the hotel and is responsible for taking care of the guests. He told us most of what I'm telling you."

"What's his name?"

"Andy something." Ned pulled a slip of paper out of his pocket. "Andy Bates. Oh, you remember the Bates Motel in *Psycho*? I hope he's not a lunatic like Norman."

We both smiled.

"I don't see how you two can joke at a time like this," said a voice behind us. A woman a bit older than Ned walked into the room. She looked like a young version of Margot.

"Professor Martindale, this is my sister, Rachel. She just got here from Seattle."

I offered my hand and received only a nod in response. She had been crying and sat down in a chair opposite her mother.

"What can this person do that the authorities aren't doing?" Rachel asked Ned. She sounded resentful, but grief does that to you, I guess.

"Rachel, I think you need to come down off your high horse and at least be civil to someone who we think might help us," said Ned.

"Help us do what? Daddy must be okay. He's just gone off to be by himself," she said. "He's done that before."

"Get real, Rachel," said Ned. "He's been gone for over two weeks."

"Maybe you're right, Rachel," said Margot, holding out her arms to her daughter.

Rachel stood up and walked over to her mother, who pulled her close and hugged her in an effort to comfort her.

"Mom, we've got to follow up on this," said Ned. "We've got to do something. You need to make up your mind about what you want to do. You asked me to invite Professor Martindale here, but if we're not going to ask him to do anything, we need to let him go home."

"I'm sorry, I know you're right. I'm just so worried about your father, I'm not thinking straight."

"Tell me what the sheriff said to you," I said.

Margot seemed to be putting her thoughts in order. Why wasn't she crying? Her composure amazed me.

"The day I first talked to the sheriff was several weeks ago—the day before Mike was to return home. I was drinking my coffee and reading the paper when the phone rang. This rather coarse voice said, 'You know someone named' . . . he paused like he was looking at some document . . . 'Michael Tateman?' I said that he was my husband, and I asked who he was. He ignored my question and just blurted out, 'He's missing somewhere up in the Steens, and we don't know where he is or if he's even alive'."

"That jerk," muttered Ned. "Didn't even have the courtesy to ask if she was sitting down or preface it with 'I have some bad news for you.' Nothing. Just the basic facts in that blunt way."

"Did he ever tell you who he was?" I asked.

Margot nodded and pulled a slip of paper from the pocket of her sweater. "Steve Murchison. He said he was the county sheriff."

"I can picture him now, riding the range and chewing tobacco when he should be investigating crimes," said Ned, anger showing in his voice. "That was no way to talk to my mom—I mean, so callous and uncaring."

"People in eastern Oregon live a lot harder life than we do here in the valley," I said, as Ned glared in disagreement with anything that seemed to be letting the sheriff off the hook. "I agree that he was too blunt but . . ."

"Maybe he was talking that way because he didn't really think that Daddy is missing, and he was . . ." Rachel's voice trailed off.

"Yeah, right," hissed Ned. "Giving Mom some tough love? Get real, Rach."

Margot appeared to be ignoring their bickering and continued. "The day after that call, Ned and I went over there," she said. "I knew I couldn't do anything, but I just had to be on the scene to get it all right in my mind."

"I can see why you'd do that," I said, trying to reassure her.

She turned to Ned. "Honey, why don't you pick up the story?"

"We got there and went to the hotel," he said. "We couldn't see Dad's room because by then someone else was staying in it. The hotel was full so the manager put us up in a newer section in the back. We couldn't even see Dad's things because the sheriff had taken them as evidence, I guess. So that seemed to be a dead end. The manager, Mr. Bates, expressed his condolences and told us that Dad stayed there one night, then hiked up on the mountain the next day, and came back and stayed another night. The next day, he walked up there again. This time he didn't return."

"When did the sheriff arrive at the hotel?" I asked.

"He pulled up about an hour after we got there," continued Ned. "We had an appointment, but he was about forty-five minutes late."

"What was he like?"

"Kind of crusty, I'd say," said Ned. "Wouldn't you agree, Mom?"

Margot nodded. "Yes, and very matter of fact."

"The operable word is blunt," added Ned.

"Did he offer any details about the investigation?" I asked. "I mean, like what they were doing?"

"He said they had organized a search involving officers from his department, which I think is pretty small," said Margot. "He talked of calling in a local rescue group and the Oregon State Police. He talked about the number of men and women who had been involved in the search and how much ground they had covered. Things like that. He mentioned setting up a command post in a trailer at the base of the mountain. His office is in Burns, about sixty miles away, so I guess having communications equipment nearby was important. It all seemed very professional to me at the time."

"He got pretty prickly when we mentioned calling in the FBI," said Ned. "He said something to my mom to the effect of 'we can handle our own cases, ma'am.' Beyond that, he wouldn't tell us a thing. He said he would keep us informed, and then he walked out and got in his car and drove away in a cloud of dust."

"Well, that shows he's looking for Daddy," said Rachel. "Maybe he's got leads he couldn't tell you about."

Ned looked angry and he started to speak, but Margot cut him off.

"I think we need more help than this sheriff can possibly give us," Margot said. She turned to me. Both she and Ned looked at me expectantly.

"You want me to look into your husband's—Mike's—disappearance?" I asked slowly.

Both Margot and Ned nodded.

"Mom told me about the other situations where you've helped your friends out. And you've known her for many years."

"Well, yeah, that's true." I was sputtering. "But I'm not a trained investigator. Friends accuse me of playing detective, but I usually botch the job and have to be rescued myself. My curiosity has almost gotten me killed more than once."

"Tom, I'm asking you to help us because you're an old friend and someone I trust," said Margot. "At first, I believed the sheriff when he talked about all of the things he was doing to find Mike. If I hadn't believed him, I would never have come home. I'd have stayed out there."

"I have to admit that the guy was pretty convincing, at first," said Ned.

"Since we got home, though, I'm beginning to have my doubts," said Margot. "He hasn't called me to report his progress.

I think he's forgotten all about us, Tom. I just don't have a lot of confidence that he will ever find Mike."

"Or that he even knows how to find him," said Ned, shaking his head.

"Don't be ridiculous," said Rachel. "He can't be that bad! He does this for a living."

"You weren't there," said Ned. "You don't know what you're talking about. Just go back to Seattle and your cushy life and take care of Bill and your kids."

"HOW DARE YOU!" she shouted. "YOU DON'T HAVE A CORNER ON CARING ABOUT WHAT MIGHT HAVE HAPPENED TO DADDY."

Margot leaned over and put an arm around Rachel. "You may not like this, but I have to do more. I know you love your dad—and me—but we've got to have more help."

Then Margot turned to me. "When I asked the sheriff how long they'd keep looking for Mike, he said he'd look until they found him. Then he mumbled something about Mike turning up. I suppose they think Mike is some rich guy from Portland who was trying to get away from it all and didn't want to be found." She paused as if to recall the scene. "I wanted to stay, but the sheriff said that my being there would hinder the search because he would have to worry about me as well as supervising the search. I wouldn't want to do that. He promised to call me periodically, but he hasn't. I'd go back now, but I wouldn't have the least idea of how to go about finding Mike. I'm not an investigator."

"Neither am I," said Ned.

"It just would not work for Ned and me to go back there right now," said Margot.

As they talked, I was considering the idea of helping them. I had promised myself and several other close friends—the ones who always had to get me out of the tight squeezes I often got into—that I would quit doing things like this.

"I'd planned to work on a book project this summer," I said, continuing to protest, albeit a bit less strenuously. "And there's the windup to my two classes. The term has two weeks to go."

The two of them sat quietly while I thought this through. After the last exchange with her brother, Rachel had left the room.

I could get Lorenzo Madrid, my attorney, to help. He has an investigator on his staff. I probably could find the time, but I didn't relish spending any money on this.

Margot read my thoughts. "I would pay you for your time, Tom," she said. "That's the least I can do. We can set up an account for your time and expenses, and you wouldn't have to go through me at all."

"I don't want any money for me," I said, "but it would be nice not to have to pay travel and other expenses. I was thinking of asking my attorney to help. He works pro bono on things, but this really doesn't qualify for that. I'm thinking of using him more as a resource person than as an attorney. He knows the law, and he also keeps an investigator on his staff. He's gotten me out of more than one bad situation. I think you'll like working with him."

Margot and Ned were smiling now. And they both looked relieved.

"So you'll do it?" said Ned.

"Yeah, I'll do it."

"Great!"

Ned jumped up and ran over to high-five me. Margot also got up and walked over to put her arms around me.

"I'm very relieved," she said. "You are so sweet to do this for us."

"Okay, great," I said. "I'll need the contact information for that sheriff and details about Mike and the car he was driving. Also, I could use a recent photo of him. Of course, you know, that phone could ring any minute with the news that he has walked into some remote ranch or ranger station and is fine."

"You may be right, of course," said Margot. "But I know Mike. He's an experienced outdoorsman. I just feel it in my bones that something bad has happened to him."

CHAPTER 11

I PULLED INTO THE SMALL PARKING LOT next to Lorenzo Madrid's office in Salem at precisely 7 p.m. He had been in court when I called from Portland, so I told his assistant to tell him I would be dropping by. Lorenzo lived for his work and much of it was good causes for which he was paid little or nothing, so he took the occasional high-profile case to put money in his bank account. He had gotten me out of jail several years ago, the same situation that was causing me some grief at the university now. He had also gotten a friend out of federal detention during a terrorism case a year ago.

I was in luck: his car was in the parking lot. I went in the front door and down the hall to his office. The walls were lined with framed awards and certificates commemorating his good work for the indigent and illegal Mexican migrants he loved to help.

"Is this the office of the biggest heartthrob in western Oregon?" I yelled before reaching his door.

Lorenzo is extremely handsome and was often mistaken for the Spanish actor Antonio Banderas. I had seen both men and women pass him slips of paper containing their phone numbers. Lorenzo refused them all. He was still grieving over the death of his lover, Scott, who had been killed several years before by a vicious gang in East Los Angeles.

"That's me, *amigo*. Come in, come in." He flashed a big smile and walked around the desk to shake my hand. "It has been far too long since I've seen you. Let me pour you some coffee."

Lorenzo loves strong coffee and buys only the best.

"I found this little coffee place here in town, and the guy knows his coffee. Gets beans from all over the world and blends them in a way that will make you cry with joy."

"That good, huh?" I took a sip. "That's MIGHTY GOOD coffee." I mimicked a radio voice.

"Sit over there," he said, gesturing to one of the chairs on the opposite side of his desk. "I feel I need some space between us— for protection." He took several gulps of coffee from a cup with the words "My attorney made me do it" on the side. "You don't usually drop in like this after hours without something on your mind—something I won't want to do, but something I will probably wind up doing because I can't resist you."

I feigned alarm. "I'm not that kind of guy," I said, laughing.

"I know, I know. Too bad for me. Okay, okay. What long-lost friend are you helping this time?"

It took me a half-hour to tell Lorenzo about the missing Mike Tateman.

"And you've known his wife a long time?"

"Thirty-five years, at least."

"So, you meet again and get together for dinner once, and she calls you during the greatest crisis of her life?"

I nodded. "You know stuff like that happens to me all the time."

He smiled. "Don't I know it. I'd have a lot more time to do my pro bono work if it wasn't for having to get you out of one mess after another. You have to agree with me on that." He shook his head as he thought back on the years of our friendship.

"Just think of it as extending your knowledge of the law beyond the typical immigration case or migrant-being-cheated-by-his-boss case." I smirked and took another gulp of coffee. "You got an innocent man—me—out of jail, and thanks to my sleuthing, you got to go to battle over the Patriot Act, right?"

"Yeah, yeah, yeah. Okay, but first I've got to ask you something, Tom. I know it will sound crude, but it is important. Do you and Margot Tateman have anything going on between you?"

"Fair question. No. Since I had my last breakup with Maxine March, I've lived the life of a monk. I suppose a psychiatrist could make a case for my getting into all the messes I get into to compensate for . . ."

"Boy, that's a breakthrough," he said laughing. "You admit that you get into messes—messes I might add that people like me have to get you out of." He hesitated for a moment and then shrugged his shoulders. "Okay, you win. I will help you, but you've got to . . . oh, never mind. I know you always break your promises when it comes to getting into trouble. What do you want me to do?"

"Great. I knew you'd see it my way." I walked over to the blackboard and picked up a piece of chalk. "Wow, you still use a blackboard and chalk."

"What do you expect me to use?"

"Never mind. It's a thing I've been going through since I went back to teaching. Everything is so high-tech now that I feel like a dinosaur."

Lorenzo stretched out both arms and extended his palms upward. "Tom, I hadn't planned to mention it, but as we say in the law biz, 'I rest my case'."

"Very funny—now, back to work," I replied. I went to the blackboard and wrote Mike Tateman's name with a box around it, Steens Mountain in another square, and drew a line between them. I put the Frenchglen Hotel and the manager's name—Andy Bates—in a box below those two and drew a line connecting all three. Then I put the name of the sheriff, Steve Murchison, in another box below all of this and ran lines from the other boxes.

"These names represent all I know," I said, putting down the chalk. "Obviously, they are connected to Mike Tateman's disappearance in some way. I guess what I'm thinking is that I should go over there and see what I can find out. I'll pose as a tourist and poke around."

"But shouldn't you wait for the official investigation to be completed?" asked Lorenzo. "At least give that sheriff a chance to do what the citizens over there elected him to do."

"That's just it—I'm not sure there is an investigation. The sheriff was pretty vague about it when Margot asked. If he did anything at all, my guess is it was pretty fast and pretty superficial."

"What do you want me to do?" asked Lorenzo. "I've got a practice to run, and it takes all of my time. I can't leave town to drive over to southeast Oregon. And, I hate to be crass, but I've got bills to pay."

"I know all of that, and I already talked it over with Margot. I gather that she's a wealthy woman. She did not hesitate when I mentioned the need to pay you. She'll pay whatever you ask, plus expenses. She wants to get this taken care of, and she trusts me to handle it. I'm not charging her anything, of course, but she'll pick up my travel expenses."

"Maybe she'll throw in a new outfit for me," said a voice from the doorway. "I'd say a little cowgirl number in suede."

I turned around and saw one of the most beautiful women I have ever seen. The yellow color of her designer suit set off her black skin perfectly.

CHAPTER 12

LORENZO GOT UP AND WALKED TOWARD THE WOMAN who, by this time, had walked several steps into the room. He grabbed her and kissed her on both cheeks. She pulled his face toward her and kissed him hard on the mouth.

"Woo hoo. I'm tryin' my best to get you to switch over to the co-ed side," she laughed, fanning herself with one hand.

Lorenzo laughed and pulled her over to me. I stood up to shake her hand.

"Tom Martindale, meet Trina Hutchins. She's my new investigator."

"Are you the professor Lorenzo's always talking about? You're cute, for an older guy," Trina said.

"Thanks, I think. I could say something about being older but wiser, but I won't."

"Yeah, don't bother. I dig older guys, so you don't have to worry."

On cue, I blushed.

"He's turnin' red, Lorenzo," she said. "That's even cuter." She looked at me. "Is that a real word?"

"I'm not on duty as a grammar policeman today."

She threw back her head and laughed loudly.

"What happened to Ray Pearl?" I asked.

"Now, he's REALLY old," said Trina. "Kind of a geezer. You should have seen his face when Lorenzo introduced me to him last week. He practically, if you'll pardon my being crude, shit a brick."

Lorenzo smiled and shook his head. "Yeah, I think it was hard for him to think that he could be replaced by anyone, let alone a pretty woman."

"And an African American woman at that!" added Trina.

"You remember the last time you were here how bad his health was getting?" said Lorenzo. "He had had emphysema for years, but it kept getting worse and now he's on oxygen. I convinced him to retire and sweetened the deal by giving him a nice bonus."

"Sounds like it was time," I said. "He did good work, but I gather you always had to put up with a lot of attitude."

"Yeah, the old New York cop in him came out most of the time," continued Lorenzo. "Those kinds of guys always sound harsh and angry even when they aren't. Their accents grate on Western ears, I think."

"How did Trina come into the picture?"

Lorenzo smiled at her as she contemplated her long fingernails.

"We were on the same legal team on a big divorce case last year. She was working for another attorney, but I got the chance to see the results of her work. She is very good at what she does."

Trina nodded in agreement without the least bit of embarrassment.

"I remembered her and called her when I finally got Ray to agree to leave," said Lorenzo. "And here she is and here you are." He gestured to both of us.

"I need to tell you, Tom, that I am more than a pretty black face," she said, guessing my thoughts about her experience. "I've been a private investigator for fifteen years. I worked first for an insurance company and then for the attorney Lorenzo mentioned."

"You don't look old enough to have worked anywhere for fifteen years," I said.

Trina laughed. "Good genes and a lot of time at the gym and various spas. I take good care of myself."

"I'm convinced," I said, as if I had ever doubted anything Lorenzo did. "I guess we need to figure out how to proceed here. I'll do anything you guys suggest."

"Anything?" Trina winked at me.

"Well, I do have a kind of morals clause in my university appointment. It's called moral turpitude."

"I'll drink to that," she said, raising her coffee cup.

CHAPTER 13

A WEEK LATER, I was heading over the Cascade Mountains on Highway 20 to eastern Oregon. I told the people in the seminar to take a week to prepare their final book proposals. That left me just the right amount of time to go to Steens Mountain and look around. Ned Tateman said he would keep me informed via cell phone if they heard anything, especially if his father was found.

Like most Oregonians who live in the most populated part of the state—along the I-5 corridor from Portland to Ashland—I do not know this vast area very well. It is very different from the Oregon that outsiders had heard of. For one thing, it doesn't rain all that much. Winters bring snow and cold, summers scorching heat. The land is what geographers call "high" desert: flat prairie with plenty of sage brush, low-growing trees, and very little water.

Politically, eastern Oregon is more conservative than the western part, and for many years, the senators and representatives in the legislature who were from there wielded most of the political power. Because the ranchers and cattlemen and attorneys from the eastern part of the state held office for many years, they were able to amass the power and influence to easily out-maneuver their more liberal counterparts with less experience and less clout from Portland or Eugene or Corvallis.

By the 1970s, however, this situation changed as more people moved into Portland and the Willamette Valley from more liberal states like California. They wanted better schools for their children and improved transportation and health care. They relied on government programs to bring this about, even if it meant higher taxes.

This philosophy was anathema to the people of eastern Oregon, who were as self-reliant as their pioneer ancestors had been during their trek to the state a hundred and fifty years before. Given the tenor of the times, however, the eastern part lost, and the people there began to suffer a long decline, due largely to hard times brought on by a decline in the housing market which reduced the need for lumber. The agriculture and cattle businesses remained strong, however.

As I considered how to find out about Mike Tateman's disappearance, I knew I'd be marked as an outsider the minute I opened my mouth. The people who live in the southeastern corner of the state are flinty and proud and no doubt suspicious of strangers. No one seen as "hifalutin" would learn more than the time of day—if that—from them.

I drove past Black Butte Ranch on the other side of the Cascades near the town of Sisters. It was developed in the 1970s as a vacation and weekend retreat for wealthy people whose primary residences are elsewhere. The homes within its gates and fences are large and expensive. I had stayed in one of them several times as a guest of one of my first students, who became a prominent Portland newspaper publisher. If my book sold a million copies and produced a major film, I *might* be able to buy a place here. Given my life style and tendency to go off chasing hopeless dreams, I doubt that a life of contemplating big skies and mountain vistas would ever materialize for me.

I headed through Sisters, which hosts an annual gathering of, you guessed it, *sisters,* along with a big quilt show. (There is also a town named Brothers in Oregon, farther east on Highway 20.)

I stopped for lunch in Bend, which had suffered more from the national housing crisis than any other city in the state. Its economy had boomed in the 1980s, 1990s, and on into the new century as Californians used the cash gained from the sale of their over-valued homes to buy cheaper houses in Bend. Now, with many of those houses unsold, the economy had suffered.

From Bend, the road to the next town of any size, Burns, was straight and long and fairly boring. At Burns, I turned south on Highway 205.

Even though it was only May, the day was hot. By 3 p.m., the outside temperature was 95 degrees, according to the thermometer gauge on the dashboard of my rental car. Each time I rolled down the window to confirm the reading, the blast of hot air made me glad I had air conditioning. Despite the intense heat, I shuddered to think of Mike Tateman, who could be either staggering around delirious or dead as one of the cow skulls laying here and there along the road, bleached white by the sun.

CHAPTER 14

Here at the Frenchglen Hotel, we are committed to being sure that your stay here is a comfortable and enjoyable one. The Hotel is a quiet wayside in a busy and hectic world. The historic hotel was originally constructed in 1916, and while it has changed a lot, primarily by a significant addition by the Civilian Conservation Corps (the CCC) in the 1930s, it remains a timeless haven for travelers some eighty-plus years later.

* * * * *

I had parked my rental car in the shade of a cottonwood tree so that I could drink some water and read a brochure about the hotel. I hadn't had trouble making a reservation because it was still late spring, a few weeks before the arrival of summer tourists. The area was popular with hikers—who liked to make the gradual ascent to the top of Steens Mountain—and nature lovers—who loved to see the hundreds of wildflowers growing in the poor soil and to glimpse the wild horses that roamed the area.

There were two cars parked in front of the hotel, but no one was sitting on the wide screened porch that I crossed to walk into the front door of the wooden building. There was no lobby, only an area with picnic-style tables with attached benches and a few chairs placed here and there along the sides. A small desk stood next to the entrance to a hall, which I presumed led to the rooms.

A woman wearing jeans, a T-shirt, and a long white apron walked in from another door to the left. "May I help you, sir?"

"Good afternoon. My name is Tom Martindale. I talked to Mr. Bates a couple of days ago and made a reservation."

"He's not here," she said. "Took a few days off before the real crunch begins. We've been open since March 15, but we don't get all that many people until about June 1."

She looked at the old-fashioned ledger on the desk and ran a finger down the lined page. "Here you are, Mr. Martingale."

"It's Martin-DALE. Not like a nightingale, which is a bird."

"What?" She looked perplexed.

"I just meant the spelling. People make that mistake because my name seems to rhyme with a bird's name."

"We get lots of bird watchers here," she said with a pleasant smile.

We really weren't getting anywhere, so I asked, "Where do I sign?"

"You really don't sign anything yet." She pushed an index card toward me. "Fill in your name and address and your car make and license number. We'll keep track of your charges beyond the room. Did he tell you it's $70 for a full-size bed?"

I nodded.

"Meals are served family style, right in here. Breakfast starts at $5.50, lunch starts at $6, and dinner costs $20 to $23. You need a reservation for that. Sometimes locals come in, and we've only got a certain number of places as you can see. Now, at this time of year, I doubt we'll be full but you never know. Our food is good, too. I help cook, and it's either chicken, pot roast, or pork chops with all the trimmings. We make all our desserts right here, and the marionberry cobbler is a house specialty."

"My mouth is watering already," I smiled.

"Now, you requested one of the newer rooms out back, I see here."

"Yeah, I have to be honest that I didn't relish the idea of using a bathroom down the hall. Those new rooms have private baths, right?"

"Yeah, they do. Some people like to rough it out here in the sticks, but I don't blame you." She handed me a key. "Shall I put you down for dinner?"

"Please. I'll see you then."

I walked back out the front door to my car, then I opened the trunk and pulled out a suitcase, my laptop, and a folder where I had been keeping notes and some printed material about Mike Tateman's disappearance—a newspaper clipping, a very fragmentary report the sheriff had sent to Margot, and some background information on the area Trina Hutchins had compiled for me. As I walked through the side yard to the new addition, a sheriff's car pulled up next to my car. Although the person behind the wheel was wearing dark glasses, I could feel his eyes watching me.

* * * * *

Several people were on the screened porch when I walked around the building two hours later. They stopped talking as I opened the door and stepped inside.

"Don't mean to be the skunk at the picnic," I said with a chuckle. "I checked in this afternoon."

"Charles Kendrick," said a tanned man with silver hair as he stuck out his hand. "We wondered what new person was joining our hearty little band." He turned to the beautiful blond woman sitting next to him, who was quite a bit younger. "My wife, Candy."

"Please, Charles. I prefer Candace."

I bowed slightly as I shook her hand. Mr. Chivalry-is-not-dead-after-all surfaced again.

"There's wine inside, by golly," said a rotund man with a red face who was sitting next to the Kendricks. An equally fat woman sat next him. Both were wearing canvas outfits with pants that ended in elastic cuffs just below the knee. The tops of their long red socks were tucked under the elastic cuffs. Pith helmets covered with netting like the kind beekeepers wear were on the table by them.

"We're the Grovers, Herb and Sue."

"Tom Martindale. Glad to meet all of you. I'm here from the valley on a short vacation. I've heard a lot about Steens Mountain, but I've never been here." I hoped that scant piece of information would get me readily accepted by the group so they would talk about themselves. I ducked inside the door, poured some white wine, and walked back outside again.

"By golly, we're old-timers here," said Herb, winking at Sue. "We've been coming up here for at least . . ." He turned to his wife. "What would you say, mother, ten years?"

"At the very least," she said, nodding her head. "At the very least."

"All kinds of birds up here, then?"

"You betcha!" answered Herb. He reached over to a briefcase on the table next to the helmets and pulled out a small booklet. "This is our life's list—we've always been lucky to fill lots of blank spaces while here. Wouldn't you say, mother?"

"I would indeed, Herb, I would indeed," said Sue, taking an extra large swig of red wine. Then she belched. "Sorry, daddy. I got some air in my throat, I guess." Then she giggled.

I turned to the Kendricks. "So, you two are civilians."

They looked perplexed, and his face turned serious.

"I made the rank of colonel, but when it seemed like there was no chance to make general, I got out. So, yes, I'm a civilian now. My wife and I are on our honeymoon."

"Oh, how sweet," said Sue, giggling and belching again.

"Mother, maybe you've had enough wine," said Herb with a worried look on his face. "I'm going to see when we're going to eat."

"I meant, as far as not being bird watchers," I was finally able to explain.

Kendrick wasn't through talking about himself. "I'm in aerospace in Southern California now. Candy—Candace—and I decided to go for a complete change of scenery for our honeymoon, so here we are." He reached over and squeezed her arm.

"Charles, you're hurting me," she said, pulling away.

That gesture seemed to anger Charles because he tightened his grip so much that the skin on her arm was all bunched up and turning red.

"And you, Mrs. Kendrick, what do you do, by golly?" Herb had rejoined our happy group.

"I was Charlie's executive assistant until a month ago when we became engaged." She held up her left hand to show us a rock the size of what F. Scott Fitzgerald had once called "a diamond as big as the Ritz."

At that moment, the cook opened the door. "Soup's on, as we say in the sticks. Dinner is ready."

The meal was as delicious as advertised. Home cooking beats gourmet fare, as far as I am concerned. Fancy food that is arranged skimpily on a plate with sauce of an unknown origin dribbled to form a flower or a butterfly or God knows what else never tastes all that good to me. Besides, you often go away hungry. This would not be the case tonight. We all dug in, Herb and Sue smacking their lips after every bite. My sentiments exactly.

As we were finishing dessert, two men and a woman walked in. One of the men had a sheriff's department uniform on. He was too young to be the man who had been so curt with Margot. The other man had to be a cowboy; he was tall and lean and wore one of those shirts with pearl snaps down the front instead of buttons. The tightness of his jeans emphasized the fact that he was bow-legged. Both men took off their wide-brimmed hats as they came inside. The young woman was hanging on tight to the arm of the cowboy. She had red hair and skin as white as milk. She also wore cowboy clothing—a shirt with pearl buttons and tight jeans. The tightness of her shirt emphasized her ample breasts, which were easily visible because the first three buttons were undone. When she took off her hat she tossed her head and her hair fell halfway down her back.

Herb's mouth was agape as he stared at the cowgirl's chest. Unfortunately for his image, a fairly large piece of cobbler was hanging from his chin. Charles Kendrick's stares were more subtle but constant. I felt movement under the table as his wife kicked him. Prude that I am, I looked once and then concentrated on my cobbler.

The three newcomers advanced to the desk, and the deputy rang the bell. The cook came through the kitchen door with a big smile on her face.

"Well, if you three aren't a sight for sore eyes," she said, pulling all of them into a group hug. "When'd you get back, Marty?"

"Early this morning, sis."

The cook turned to the rest of us. "He's my baby brother, and this is Lurlene, his fiancée. The other big brute is her brother, Clay. Marty's been working on a big cattle ranch in Nevada."

We nodded and murmured our greetings. The three looked in our direction briefly, and then turned back to the cook. I am sure she had done this countless times with countless guests at the hotel and it was boring, and for her brother, embarrassing.

"Are we late for dinner?" asked Marty. "I haven't eaten all day and neither has Lurlene. How 'bout you, Clay—you had anything?"

The deputy shook his head as the cook motioned them to a table at the other end of the room. It seemed to me that he staggered a bit as he walked.

"I've got plenty left," the cook said. "These nice folks barely made a dent in what I fixed."

All of us went back to what we were talking about, although in hushed tones now that we had an audience beyond our table.

"I like to rough it once in a while," said Kendrick. "I mean, with drinking coffee around the campfire and bathing in an icy stream. It's such a change from the way I usually live that it helps me figure out what's important in life."

"How about you, Candace?" I asked. "Do you enjoy a life in the wild?"

"Good God, no," said Kendrick, before his wife could open her mouth. "Candy's idea of roughing it would be to sleep in one of those huge tents they set up on African safaris with Persian rugs on the floor and hot and cold running servants."

Candace Kendrick glared at him but did not say anything.

"My kind of camping," I said, cheerfully, trying to defuse the tense situation my question had caused.

"So, I guess we got ourselves some big city sissies."

The voice came from the other table. The deputy had turned around so that he was facing in our direction. Marty and Lurlene had their heads down as they ate. All of us ignored the taunt, but the deputy was not giving up.

"I SAID, WE GOT OURSELVES A BUNCH . . ."

"Let it be, Clay," said Marty. "Eat your supper."

The cook rushed over to our table. "Did you all get enough to eat? There's a lot more cobbler if you want some."

Herb started to open his mouth, but his wife interrupted. "We are stuffed. We need to get to bed and get our beauty sleep, so we'll be ready for more bird watching in the morning."

"You know what, Marty, I think beauty sleep would be lost on that fat cow."

In seconds, Herb jumped to his feet and was standing over the deputy.

"You insulted my wife," he said. "Take it back, or I'm going to have to ask you to step outside."

The deputy stood up. He had to be over six feet tall, so he towered over Herb. "What'd you say, little fella? How is it in bed with a fat cow like that? Do you get lost in the folds of her skin?"

At this point, I grabbed Herb as Marty grabbed the deputy.

"LET ME AT HIM," shouted Herb. "I'll kill him."

I got Herb into a chair next to his wife, who was crying and rubbing his arm. Candace Kendrick stood behind them, patting them on their shoulders.

Marty had pulled Clay back to his chair and had knelt down beside him. He was talking in a hushed tone, but I could hear most of what he was saying.

"What the fuck is the matter with you? You been drinkin' on duty again. The sheriff will have your ass, and I won't be able to help you this time. Don't you know how much this town depends on people like them? We need their money. You know, Clay, sometimes you don't have the sense of a donkey."

Lurlene had remained seated during the entire fracas, her face without expression.

Marty walked over to me and said, "I'm sorry about all of this, mister . . ."

"Tom Martindale."

We shook hands.

"My soon-to-be brother-in-law has had too much rotgut wine, I'm afraid. He got into trouble a couple of months ago for drinking on the job. Sheriff Murchison's going to be real pissed that he's been at it again. He's his uncle, and they're very close, but he can't keep excusing Clay and covering up stuff when he screws up."

"What he said was way out of line," I said. "For anybody, but definitely for someone who is supposed to uphold the law. Just get him out of here and keep him away from us. It'll probably blow over. I really don't know any of these people . . . met them just today . . . but we'll all be gone in a day or two. As I say, though, just get him out of here and sober him up."

I turned to the others. "I guess the deputy had too much to drink."

"That's no excuse for that kind of trash talk," said Sue.

We all nodded in agreement.

Behind us, I could hear chairs scraping. I turned around to see Marty and Lurlene supporting Clay between them as they walked out the front door.

"Very unpleasant incident," said Kendrick, turning to his wife. "What's say we head for bed?"

"You okay, Herb?" I asked. "I don't think he'll bother us any more. Marty, the cowboy, promised to keep him in line."

We all shook hands and the four of them headed down the hall and up the stairs to their rooms. I walked outside and down the steps. As I crossed the yard, I heard the low murmur of a car idling. I quickened my pace and unlocked the door of my room. Before going inside, I turned in time to see a sheriff's patrol car slowly pull away and drive down the highway.

CHAPTER 15

I BEAT EVERYONE INTO THE DINING ROOM the next morning so I could be on my way without having to speak to anyone. I like people, but I have lived alone long enough to enjoy my own company. As my grandmother used to say, "Solitude is better than bad company."

I met Herb and Sue as I walked out the door. They were so busy writing in their life list of birds the ones they had seen that they almost bumped into me.

"You guys are out early," I said. "I thought I was the only one up."

"Oh goodness," said Sue with a startled look on her face. "You scared me half to death!"

"It's a great morning out there, by golly," said Herb, his eyes glowing. "We saw a Caspian tern."

"There are twenty-two species of ducks at the Malheur National Wildlife Refuge near here," added Sue. "I think we've added fourteen of them to our lists since we've been coming up here."

I suppose their quest was no different from collecting items of a more prosaic nature—like stamps or coins or, in my case, books.

"That is great," I said. "You must be thrilled."

"By golly, we are feelin' pretty good, all right," said Herb. "Where you off to?"

"I'm just going to drive around to see the area," I said. "I don't have any special destination. This whole area fascinates me. I had no idea it was so beautiful. I've never been that fond of wide open spaces."

"I hope you don't run into that deputy," said Sue, her eyes filling with tears. "He is mean."

"That bastard," said Herb. "I'd have liked to whip his ass, by golly. And I would have if you hadn't held me back."

"I'm sorry that happened," I said to both of them. "It was uncalled for, stupid really. I guess he'd been drinking, but that's no excuse."

"I'd watch out for him, Tom," said Herb, lowering his voice and glancing toward the kitchen. "He'd as soon write you a ticket as look at you."

"I'll bet he's sleeping it off this morning," I laughed. "Well, I'll bid you folks a good morning and be on my way. Not sure if I'll make it back for lunch, but I'll see you at dinner."

I drove south on Highway 205 and turned left toward Steens Mountain. Although it is possible to drive the entire 9,000 feet to the top, I had been told that snow could make the road impassable before I reached the top. Even though it was mid-May, the sun wasn't strong enough to melt the snow. I decided to drive as far as I could to get an idea of the mountain, then get out and walk around. This was, after all, a kind of reconnaissance mission for me. I would come back in a few weeks for the serious stuff. Margot would have to realize that this kind of thing takes time. There was also the possibility that the sheriff would figure out what happened to Mike and I could go back to my writing.

At about the 3,000 foot level, the road ahead was blocked by deep snow. I vowed to rent a vehicle with four-wheel drive next time. Even without the snow, the gravel road was full of potholes and there were places where it had vanished altogether. Given all the flying gravel, I was glad I had left my own car at home. The windshield and paint job would have been ruined by this time.

I stopped at a place where the road had widened and turned around. I could park here safely because anyone coming up or down could clearly see the car. I started walking up the road toward the summit, carefully picking my way through the snow-drifts. I hoped my boots would keep my feet warm and dry. I buttoned up my heavy parka and put on my wool hat. I was as ready as any city boy could ever be for a trek into the wilderness.

I climbed for about a half-hour without making a lot of progress, given the deep snow. At this point, there was little evidence of the magnificent views I had heard about—rocky terrain and a few scrubby trees were all I saw on either side of me. If Mike Tateman had come this way, there would be no evidence of it until the late spring thaw. After another fifteen minutes, I decided that the summit would have to wait for a month or so. As I started back toward the car, a sudden shaft of light glanced across my face. I kept walking and the light flashed again. I looked in that direction in time to see that the beam was caused by the reflection of the sun on a lens. A telescope? A gun sight? I hurried along.

A few minutes later, I looked down to see the light from a laser shining on my chest, so I quickly ducked behind a large rock and waited for a bullet to whiz by my head. I waited and strained to hear the sound of someone walking toward me or cocking a rifle, but it was quiet, except for the persistent buzzing of a fly that kept landing on my nose.

I waited another ten minutes before running the last few yards to the car, expecting to be shot with every step I took. I got in the car, started the engine, and drove down the mountain as fast as the potholes would allow.

* * * * *

That afternoon, after asking the cook to fix me a sandwich, I drove down the highway in the opposite direction to look for wild horses. Thousands of wild horses have roamed the West for years. Some are descended from Indian ponies; others from the horses that early ranchers kept to work their huge spreads. It is said that the ranchers did not break or tame them until they needed them. Today, the remaining herds of wild horses are managed by the Bureau of Land Management, an agency of the United States Department of Interior. For reasons of public relations, none of them are ever killed and some are offered for adoption.

I drove to the Kiger Wild Horse Viewing Area and parked. As I had been warned might be the case, there were no horses in sight. I decided to walk toward a grove of trees to see if any were visible away from the road. Although the ground was uneven, I reached the trees quickly. Ahead of me was a creek that formed a pond, and around the pond were ten of the most beautiful horses I had ever seen. Red roans and black-and-white and brown-and-white mustangs drank quietly from the pond, only a few glancing in my direction. A big stallion stood guard over the others and trotted toward me as if warning me to stay away.

I tried not to move except to lift my camera slowly up into position. At the whir of its shutter, the horses all looked up and began racing away from the pond.

"Now you've gone and scared my horses away," said a voice from behind me. I did not turn but put my hands in the air as I heard a rifle being cocked.

CHAPTER 16

"LOWER YOUR ARMS," said the voice. "You don't look all that dangerous to me. You can turn around."

A man, who looked to be in his sixties, was mounted on a huge black horse. He was dressed like a cowboy—a cowboy out of the pages of a Ralph Lauren ad. His jeans and shirt and suede jacket looked expensive and well cared for. His wide-brimmed hat was circled by a beaded band. His shirt was set off by a bolo tie, held in place by a large turquoise stone set in silver.

He lowered his rifle and got off his horse. "Dickson White." He extended his hand and we shook.

"Tom Martindale."

"I know everyone who lives around here and I don't know you," he said. "Mind telling me where you're from and what you're doing on my land?"

"I'm a visitor. Staying at the Frenchglen Hotel. I got in yesterday and thought I'd look around this morning. I didn't get very far when I tried to drive up the mountain so I drove this way. I saw the wild horse viewing area and stopped to look. There were none in sight, so I wandered into these trees. I thought this was a government refuge. I didn't know it was private property. I'm sorry."

"That's okay," said White. "Private and public are all tangled up around here. We don't pay much attention to that. I do my thing and they do theirs, but they leave me alone. The less government interferes with us, the better we like it."

"So, did you think I was some kind of government agent?" I asked.

"No, not really. It's just that we don't get a lot of strangers around here—I mean on my ranch."

"You don't get any tourists to see the horses?"

White's eyes narrowed and he frowned. "Why you askin' all the questions? You takin' a survey or something?"

I made a wide sweep of my arms, palms pointing down. "No, not at all." Time to change the subject. "Those horses are really something to see. Makes me think of that old song, 'Born Free.' But I guess that applied to African lions."

I was babbling and White was looking skeptical.

"I won't keep you," I said. "Thanks for . . ."

"Not shooting you for trespassing."

"Something like that, yes. I'll be more careful next time."

"Next time? I thought you were just passing through."

"A figure of speech," I said, trying to keep from sounding nervous. "I'm leaving tomorrow."

White got up on his horse and wheeled it around. Without glancing in my direction, he nudged the animal on its sides and it trotted off. I won't say I did the same thing to get back to my car, but I did walk pretty fast.

* * * * *

"Help yourself to the pot roast and mashed potatoes," said the cook, as I joined the other four guests at the table.

"Sorry to be late. I dozed off and just woke up. All of this country air has relaxed me to the point where I'm sleepy all the time."

"You got *that* right," said Kendrick. "I can't stay awake either, when we go to bed, and my beautiful wife doesn't much like it, do you Candy?"

His wife blushed, and Sue and Herb looked uncomfortable.

"That is TMI—'too much information,' in the vernacular of my students," I said.

"Well, by golly, this meat looks mighty good," said Herb, in a swift change of subject. "Mighty good."

I helped myself to two slices of beef and a big dollop of potatoes.

"Salad dressing?" asked Sue.

"Great. Thanks."

All conversation stopped as we began to eat. In a bit, I asked, "What did you all do today?"

"We went looking for those Caspian terns," said Sue. "Those little devils are hard to find."

"You'd better believe it, by golly," said Herb.

"We drove into Burns," said Kendrick. "I had to send a fax to my office, and the one at the hotel is broken. No rest for the weary."

"Or the wicked," I said with a wink directed to Candace.

She smiled at first, but her husband's dirty look brought any levity to an end.

"How about you, Tom?" said Sue. "What did you do with yourself all day?"

I cleaned my plate and dabbed at my mouth with a napkin. "I tried to drive up the mountain, but I didn't get very far. The snow on the road made it impossible to go much higher than about 3,000 feet. I don't have four-wheel drive on the rental car so that was that. I got out and looked around a bit, but the cold made me scurry back to the car pretty fast."

I decided not to mention either encounter—with whoever had trained the rifle scope on me and the Ralph Lauren rancher.

After dinner, the five of us sat around the table drinking coffee.

"You know, Tom, you never told us much about yourself the other night, except for where you live," said Sue. "What do you do?"

Egotist that I am, I hate to talk about myself. If forced to do so, I give a much abbreviated synopsis.

"Yeah, I guess we got sidetracked by that idiotic deputy. I taught journalism at Oregon University for more years than I care to admit. Before that, I had a career as a magazine journalist working out of New York. Recently, I've been on leave for a few years to write a book and . . ."

"You academic guys really slay me," said Kendrick. "You only teach a few hours a week and then you still take a lot of time off, like to write bullshit books that nobody reads. In business, we have to work hard for what we make." He emptied his wine glass and filled it again.

His wife looked like she could kill him before becoming invisible. I decided not to dignify what he said by rising to the bait. Well, almost anyway.

"Yeah, I guess it seems that way to nonacademics. I know we've never met a payroll or been able have our pick of the steno pool or . . ."

Kendrick jumped to his feet and took a swing at me. I ducked just in time, and he fell back onto the bench. He would have toppled over backwards had his wife not grabbed his back. I stood up.

"Must be a full moon tonight," I said. "I'm going to go to bed. I've got an early start in the morning. It's been good meeting all of you." I glanced at Kendrick, who had put his head on the table. "Most all of you."

The other three got up, and we shook hands. Candace Kendrick stepped away to lean over to me.

"Charlie drinks too much," she whispered. "This isn't the first time his mouth has gotten him into trouble. I'm sorry."

"No, no. I want to apologize to you," I said. "That was a cheap shot, but I needed to put him in his place. You are a lovely person, and he's lucky to have you as his wife."

She nodded. "Thanks," she said. "By the way, he didn't get me out of the steno pool. I came into his company from a temp agency."

* * * * *

I skipped breakfast and left Frenchglen a little after seven, since I had paid my bill the night before. I drove for about a half-hour and kept checking my cell phone to see if I had coverage. Just outside Burns, the phone finally showed some bars. I punched in a familiar number.

"Margot. It's Tom. Did I wake you?"

"Tom. Good to hear your voice. What time is it?"

"About 7:30. You want me to call back? The reason I called so early is to report what I've found out. There's no cell phone coverage in Frenchglen, so this is the first chance I've had to contact you."

"No, don't worry. I don't sleep all that well these days. What's been happening?"

"I don't have a lot to report. There's so much snow, I didn't get to poke around the mountain like I planned to do. I've met some of the people here and know the territory, so I can get around better when I come back. I also know what to have Lorenzo and his investigator look for. I'll fill you in on all of this when I see you."

"Any sign of a search going on? I mean men on horseback with tracking dogs or something like that?"

"No, nothing like that. I didn't want to ask any questions. I didn't want people to know what I was looking for. This is such a small town that everyone knows everything instantly."

"I can't hear you very well," she said, over a line that was increasingly filled with static.

"You're breaking up. I'll call you tomorrow."

I drove into Burns in another half-hour. On the spur of the moment, I decided to talk to someone I could speak with candidly. Jeff Walls had been a student of mine ten years before. After a few years with the Associated Press, he had returned to his home town and bought the weekly newspaper, the *Burns Beacon*.

The front door had one of those bells on it to indicate that someone had entered. A heavy-set woman looked up from her computer as I stepped inside.

"Yes, sir. How may I help you?"

"Good morning. Is Mr. Walls here?"

"JEFF! SOME MAN HERE TO SEE YOU!" she yelled toward the back, then turned to me and said, "I'm sure he'll be right out."

Along with the dead from the city cemetery, I thought to myself. "Thanks."

I walked over to a rack in the corner where recent issues were displayed. The tabloid-sized paper was impressive looking: good typefaces and clean design. Not your usual back-country weekly.

"I can't believe it," said a voice from behind me. "It's great to see you."

We hugged and patted each other on the back. The woman at the computer looked a bit shocked at this display of manly affection. I guess that kind of thing wasn't done over here.

Jeff turned to the woman. "Marcella, this is my journalism teacher from college. He taught me everything I know."

"Pleased to meet ya." She stood up and shook my hand.

"My pleasure, ma'am."

"Oh, it's **Marcella**, please. This young squirt talks about you all the time."

"I'm not young anymore, and I'm not a squirt. Marcella's my aunt. She's helped me here at the paper since my mom and dad died."

"I'm sorry," I said. "I remember meeting them on a Mom's Weekend at school when you were a senior. Great people. What happened?"

"A car accident," said Jeff, a sad look on his face. "Even though we don't have many cars out here in the boonies, people still manage to run into one another. Two winters ago, when they were coming back from a vacation in Arizona, they hit a patch of ice and rolled over in front of a semi that was barreling down the highway. Mercifully, I don't think they knew what hit them."

Marcella dabbed at her eyes and blew her nose.

"But you didn't come all this way to hear about my sad life," he said. "Come on back to my office. The paper just came out so I've got a fairly free day. We'll talk and then have some lunch. They make a pretty good burger over at the Cattlemen's Café."

Jeff told me about buying the paper five years ago with financial help from his parents. He had grown sick of the rat race that working for a wire service inevitably becomes. After living in Detroit and Houston, he tried for an overseas assignment. When he didn't get it, he decided to come home and to achieve the dream that many people in journalism strive for: his own newspaper. Even though the *Burns Beacon* had a small reader and advertising base, it wasn't doing all that badly. Truth be told, weeklies with no competition thrived these days because people have no place else to turn for their news.

"So you've got a little gold mine here," I said, taking a sip of coffee.

"Hardly, but I can't complain." He looked at his watch. "If we leave now, we can beat the crowd at the Cattlemen's."

* * * * *

We had polished off our burgers and milk shakes and were about to tackle apple pie and coffee when a big man in a uniform walked over to the table.

"Sheriff," said Jeff, reaching over to shake the big man's hand.

"You goin' to introduce me to your friend here, Jeff?"

"Oh, sure. Sorry. Sheriff Steve Murchison, this is my old professor from the university, Tom Martindale."

I extended my hand, but he did not shake it.

"You're kind of out of your element here, professor. Tryin' to see how the other half lives?"

"I'm just passing through on a short vacation. Jeff was one of my best students, and I thought I'd see how he was doing." I returned to my pie and coffee.

"He taught me everything I know," said Jeff, cheerfully.

"And what would that be?"

His hostility surprised me, but I kept smiling.

"It would maybe fill a thimble," I said.

The sheriff did not crack a smile, but Jeff laughed out loud.

"You comin' or goin'?" the sheriff asked me.

"I'm leaving town this afternoon, heading home. I've been up to Steens Mountain."

"Oh, so you were with that bunch up there the other night." He turned toward the front of the café, and I saw his foul-mouthed deputy standing there looking at us.

"If you mean that I was a guest at the Frenchglen Hotel, you're right," I said. "But I guess your deputy already told you that. I have to tell you that he got pretty drunk and was pretty obnoxious to some of the guests."

"Is that so? Well, we call 'em like we see 'em, out here in the sticks. We're not all that gen-teel, like you guys from the big city. Nice meetin' you. I don't 'spose we'll be seein' you again."

"Likewise. Oh, you never know where I'll turn up."

The sheriff walked to the front of the café, and he and his deputy walked out the door.

"What was **that** all about?" asked Jeff.

"The first night I got there, I was having dinner with the four other guests at the hotel and this guy, Clay something or other— I didn't get his last name . . ."

"Murchison," said Jeff. "He's the sheriff's nephew."

"Yeah, I guess I heard that. Anyway, this guy walked in with another guy—a cowboy—and a very pretty girl. They were there for supper and sat down at a table on the other side of the room. We were minding our own business and talking among ourselves when this guy Clay proceeded to insult one of the ladies, calling her a fat slob and stuff like that. Her husband went for him, but I pulled him back and the cowboy pulled the deputy back. They left, and we broke it up pretty quickly too. He had ruined our evening."

"That's really awful," said Jeff. "Clay's been that way all his life. A real hothead. I went all through school with him, and he's always been in trouble. He and another delinquent—a rich man's son named Junior White—have terrorized this area for years."

"Would he be related to Dickson White?"

"He's his son. How'd you know about him?"

I explained my encounter with the older White while I was looking at the wild horses.

"Good thing he didn't shoot you," said Jeff, shaking his head. "He thinks he's the law around here and does pretty much anything he wants. He owns most of the private land and because the federal land is interspersed with it, he acts like he owns it all. The BLM doesn't want to cause trouble, so they don't cross him. He gives a lot of money to the Republican Party, so he can count on help from local and national officials. If something makes him mad, he has no qualms about complaining. And he always gets his way."

"You boys want some more pie?" The waitress had returned.

Jeff looked at his watch. "I guess I need to get back to work. Even though I'm the boss, my aunt will make a big deal about my long lunch."

I picked up the check, but Jeff grabbed it from my hand.

"My treat," he said smiling. "After all you did for me when I was at the university, it's the least I can do."

We walked back to the office and in the door. His aunt grabbed her purse and headed out the door before we could close it.

"Nice to be able to keep banker's hours," she said. "Your messages are on your desk."

We walked into his office, and he pointed to the chair opposite his desk.

"I need to get on the road," I said. "But before I go, I want to talk to you about something else." I looked behind me. "Something I'd just as soon no one else hears, even your aunt."

"Especially my aunt. I love her dearly and I don't know what I'd do without her, but she's a terrible gossip." He got up and closed his office door. "I can hear the bell if anyone comes in." He sat down again. "Okay, Tom. I'm all ears."

Over the next hour or so I told Jeff about Mike Tateman's disappearance in the Steens area and how Margot had asked me to look into it because the sheriff did not seem all that interested in finding out what had happened to her husband.

"That surprises me," Jeff said. "Murchison is a real pain in the ass and a nasty cuss, but I never doubted that he was a fairly good cop. He does have to face reelection every few years, and that won't happen if he doesn't do his job. You don't think he's done anything to find your friend's husband?"

"Not that he's told her about. And besides, wouldn't you have heard about any large-scale investigation? I mean, there would have been search teams and tracking dogs and even planes flying over the area."

"Yeah, you're right. When did this guy go missing?"

"Less than a month ago."

"Of course, the weather was bad then," said Jeff. "We had a very heavy snow kind of late in the season, and it stuck around for a while. And visibility was bad up until a week ago."

"I think all of this needs to be investigated," I said. "And Margot—my old friend—asked me to look into this. She's beside herself with grief, and then she finds out that this local sheriff appears to be ignoring the whole thing. God, she can't even have a funeral or a memorial service."

"With all due respect, Tom, why did she ask you?"

"Fair question. I've gone out on a limb for friends a couple of times over the past few years. I won't bore you with the details, but I have been successful because I'm dogged about it."

"What do you plan to do?"

"Now that I have an idea of how things are here, I plan to come back and stay longer with the hope that I can find out what happened to Mike Tateman."

Jeff whistled and shook his head. "It might be dangerous. This is still the wild West in many ways. People shoot first and ask questions later, and they often get away with the bad things they do. I mean, look at Clay and Junior White, the rich man's son I told you about. You may need to bring in some outside law enforcement people."

"I plan to try to do that, but I need some evidence first that Mike is even missing. You know the drill: the authorities usually say that a missing person has gone off on his own for personal or other reasons—or has committed suicide."

"Murchison said that?"

"No, not yet, but I'll bet he's going to say that if push comes to shove. Margot hasn't pressured him up to this point. She's been waiting to see what I find out."

"What can I do?"

"No, no. You can't get involved in this, Jeff. You've got a lot at stake—your paper, your reputation. It could get ugly if I find out that local bigwigs—like the sheriff or even Dickson White—were involved in Mike's disappearance. It has been my experience that people like that will do anything to cover up the bad stuff they do."

Jeff thought for a moment. "No, I'm in. I'll sniff around under the guise of doing my job. I can nose around more easily than you can. You're an outsider, and we country hicks are always suspicious of outsiders. And you're maybe even a liberal!"

"I plead guilty to that." I smiled. "Okay, okay. I'm happy to let you help us, but I want you to promise me that you won't take any chances. Just do some preliminary research, and let me know what you find out. I'll do the rest, along with some help from my attorney, Lorenzo Madrid, and his investigator."

I stood up and shook Jeff's hand. "Here's my card. Call me anytime. I need to get on the road. I've got to wind up two classes and then I'll be back here, depending on what you find out." I looked him in the eye. "Now, think this through. Do you really want to do this?"

Jeff looked excited. "Now more than ever. Besides, you know as well as I do that this will make a terrific story and it will be exclusive to the *Burns Beacon*. It'll put my little rag on the map."

CHAPTER 17

NOTES FROM THE CLASS FROM HELL

As usual, the students in my careers class paid scant attention when I took my place behind the lectern in the front of the room. I had abandoned the use of a lectern years ago but had gone back to using it to keep this mob at bay.

"I can't say that I will miss you as a class," I said to get their attention. Most of them looked up and, miraculously, stopped texting. "Almost without exception, you have ignored the speakers from various mediums of communication that I have brought in to speak to you each week, in the apparently mistaken belief that any of you actually want a career in what is still laughingly referred to as journalism."

I had them now, when it was too late. But, no matter, I was on a roll so I continued. "I leave you with a warning about this profession. It has changed so much in the past few years that I doubt I could get a job today. The old parts of this business that I worked in—newspapers and magazines—are either no longer in existence or so changed that I would not know how to function even if I could get a job. What has come to be called 'social media'—what you so rudely do on your Blackberries or iPhones in this classroom every time we meet—seems to have taken the place of traditional media outlets. This is because of people like you. You believe what some obscure blogger without any training says instead of someone who has studied how to write and edit and knows about the laws of libel and codes of ethics."

"So what chance do we have at finding jobs?" asked Samuel, the African American student who had talked the first day.

As I thought about my answer, I looked at the one student whose attitude had gotten to me all term: the rich girl Tina Alsop. She had not stopped texting the whole time I had been talking. I walked toward her and kept talking. The students were all watching me carefully.

"The irony is, you will probably do fine because you are as scattered as the media you are joining."

I stopped at her desk. I took her device away from her and put it in my pocket.

"You know, I've wanted to do this all term," I said. "You haven't stopped your texting for one minute. I'm not sure why you even come to class. If you stayed away, you could keep in touch with your boyfriend or family or whoever you are so keen on texting a lot more."

She batted her eyes a few times and then stared at me without a word. "I'll give this back to you at the end of class," I said, triumphantly.

"What. Ever." Then she pulled out another cell phone from her designer handbag and resumed texting.

* * * * *

"I've missed getting together with all of you this past week," I said to the book writing class. "I can't believe the term is nearly over, and you're ready to present your final book proposals today. I'm anxious to hear about them and read them."

Peter Ogle went first, hesitant and shy when he started, more forceful as he got into the subject he knew so well.

He concluded: "With thoughts of the punishment the army would no doubt subject me to for disobeying the now-dead lieutenant, I jumped down from the APC and ran toward the car. As I neared the car, I saw that it was a large Mercedes. The person who owned it has money, I thought, or was it stolen from a wealthy person in Kuwait? Would it be filled with military officers fleeing the American invasion or stolen art or jewelry or even bundles of cash? I walked toward the driver's side of the car, which was still burning. Even at the risk of being blown up myself, I had to know who we had killed. The driver was slumped over the steering wheel, his distorted face a mass of blood. I peered in the smashed window and saw the body of a small boy—maybe seven or eight—sitting next to the driver. His small hand was gripping the hand of the driver. I turned and ran back to our vehicle, wiping the tears from my eyes."

As before, when Ogle discussed his book idea the first day of class, everyone was crying, including me and Ned, who had arrived midway through the reading.

"What can I say, Peter?" I said after a few moments. "Very powerful stuff. Why don't we take a short break."

Ogle and the three women clustered around Ned, welcoming him back and offering condolences, then they walked outside and Ned sat down beside me.

"Mom says you found out a few things down in the Steens," he said. "I'm anxious to hear about it. Any leads on where my dad is?"

I shook my head. "No, I didn't have a chance to actually look for him. Weather was bad and time was short."

The door opened and the other students filed back in.

"Drop by my office after class, and I'll fill you in."

"Great. Mom's not doing very well. She needs to hear some news, even if it isn't good."

I turned to the class. "Peter will be the proverbial tough act to follow. Who wants to go next?"

Kate raised her hand and presented a well-written proposal about her rape and the case histories of the other women she was profiling. Amanda was next with her book idea about baby beauty pageants. It was also well done and, I suspected, very saleable.

That left Gertrude Snyder, who had been nervously shuffling her papers since class began.

"Okay, Gertrude, you're on," I said cheerfully. The five of us looked at her expectantly, and she burst into tears.

"I can't do it," she sobbed. "I can't keep up with all of you. I'm too old to become a writer. I should have stayed home and tended to my knitting."

As before, both Kate and Amanda, who were sitting on either side of her, reached over and put their arms around her. Gertrude was right in her self-assessment but I was not about to agree with her. If I said anything that was not supportive, I would crush what little self-esteem she had left. And what purpose would that serve?

"Gertrude, there is no shame in taking more time to finish your proposal," I said. "You haven't been in school for a while, but you know we have what is called an 'I' grade. That's for 'Incomplete.' I will be happy to give you that so you can continue to work on your proposal this summer. I'm going to be out of town a lot on another project . . ." I glanced at Ned, "but I can check with you from time to time and see how you're doing."

"You would do that?" sobbed Gertrude, blowing her nose and dabbing at her eyes.

"I can help too," said Kate Knowland.

"And me too," said Amanda Morrison. "We'll both be taking classes this summer."

"That is really good of you both," I said, as Gertrude nodded her head in agreement. I held back a bit because, as much as I wanted to help Gertrude, I did not want to wind up fielding her calls and visits to my office all summer. I knew from experience that you could never give the Gertrudes of the world enough time, and I just would not have the time. I asked the others to polish off their book proposals and give them back to me so I could forward them to my agent.

✳ ✳ ✳ ✳ ✳

A few minutes later in my office, I directed Ned to a chair.

"Your mom is not doing very well? I haven't called her."

He sighed. "Nah, she just can't shake off her depression."

"Of course, I don't blame her. She must feel very helpless."

"I talked her into going up to Seattle to stay with my sister for a while," he said. "My sister has two kids, and they'll keep my mom hopping. They're pretty lively."

"Sounds like a good plan. Okay, let me tell you what I've found out so far." It took me an hour to bring Ned up to date on my trip. "So, that's where things stood when I left there to finish up these courses and let the snow melt."

"Your former student . . ."

"Jeff Walls."

"Yeah, Jeff. He's willing to do all of this work for us?"

"He volunteered to do it. I didn't ask."

"I don't mean to sound ungrateful, but why would he do that for people he doesn't know."

"Part of it is loyalty to me, I think," I said. "And the other part is his love for pursuing a good story. You aren't a reporter, so it may be hard for you to understand. When you've got that in your genes, you can't slough off what others would ignore. I'm the same way. That's one of the reasons I'm helping you and your mother, along with our friendship."

Ned nodded, but still looked a bit skeptical.

"Well, whatever the reason, I'm grateful to you both," he said. "Be sure to tell him to keep track of his expenses. We, I mean my mom, will want to reimburse him."

"I'll tell him."

"I'm going to get out of here so you can get on with your day." Ned stood up and extended his hand. "Thank you very much for all you're doing." He wiped a tear from an eye. "My dad is dead, I'm pretty sure about that, but we've got to find out how and why."

"I'll do my best."

* * * * *

I was finished with the two courses a few days later. Since both were courses without final exams, I could get my grades in early. I would grade the class from hell—the careers course—on attendance. Since all the students had been there—along with their iPhones and bad attitudes—I really couldn't give them the low grades they deserved. I had learned long ago that a professor couldn't grade a student down just because he or she was unpleasant. If they did the work, you had to grade on that. These kids had been in class, but they hadn't responded to me or the guest speakers. They just filled the seats, for the most part. So, I decided to consider class participation in my grading. On that score, I gave most of them a C. I could justify that, even for Tina Alsop. I had learned long ago that you can't give out grades punitively.

The book writing class was a different story. For these five students, I factored in the quality and depth of their book proposals and their participation. All four of them had been there every day and spoken often, asking me good questions and giving thoughtful suggestions to each other. I gave Gertrude Snyder the "Incomplete" we had discussed. I hoped she would finish her project.

I felt good as I filled out the grade sheet. They deserved their A's. Given all the distractions in his life, Ned had also asked for an "Incomplete," which I was happy to give him.

Later that day, I cleared out my apartment and drove back to the coast. I would be working from my house there all summer, except when I was tramping around Steens Mountain.

CHAPTER 18

THE NEXT MORNING, I began to construct a timeline for Mike Tateman's disappearance. I jotted down the various dates and people involved on index cards, which I attached to a bulletin board with push pins. At first, I could add only the day he left for the Steens and the day I figured he checked into the hotel. A pretty skimpy amount of information to go on, but I knew there'd be many more cards on the board before very long.

That afternoon, I received an e-mail from Jeff Walls in Burns with a lot of attachments. His message was brief: "FYI. Lots of things to check on." The attachments were mostly links to newspaper websites that he had found through the key words "Dickson White."

One only had to read the headlines to trace the trajectory of a successful man.

DICKSON WHITE ELECTED TO STATE SENATE
WHITE NAMED TO GOVERNOR'S WATER COUNCIL
DICKSON WHITE TO HEAD CATTLEMEN'S ASSOCIATION
DICKSON WHITE RECEIVES HONORARY DEGREE

DICKSON WHITE TO HEAD OREGONIANS FOR NIXON
WHITE TO CO-CHAIR BUSH RE-ELECTION CAMPAIGN
WHITE DONATES $1 MILLION TO ORAL ROBERTS UNIV.

The list of stories on White and his life ran five screens long. Interspersed with all the good stuff, however, was a bit of the bad.

DICKSON WHITE JR. ARRESTED IN DRUG BUST
DICKSON WHITE JR. CHARGED WITH RAPE
NOTED DEFENSE ATTORNEY HIRED FOR EASTERN OR.
  MAN
WHITE JR. STEALS MOTHER'S JEWELRY FOR DRUG BUY
WHITE JR. GETS PROBATION FOR RAPE CHARGE
WHITE JR. ENTERS CALIF. TREATMENT CENTER

Even the mighty have skeletons in their closets, I thought to myself as I read the stories. The trajectory of the life of White's son ran in the opposite direction of his own. I wrote the names of both Dickson White and Dickson White Jr. on cards and put them up on the bulletin board. I had no need to print out the stories, but the information in them might help solve the puzzle of Mike Tateman's disappearance.

I looked up Steve Murchison, the local sheriff, and found little of interest. The stories about him dealt mainly with his statements regarding various people who had been arrested for various crimes over the years, plus his annual appearance before the county board of commissioners to ask for more money.

One last story caught my eye.

IT'S ALL IN THE FAMILY FOR SHERIFF AND NEPHEW

The feature story about the sheriff used the news peg of his nephew Clay, hired as his deputy. Buried deep in the piece were these sentences:

Clay Murchison grew up in the Steens Mountain area where he was befriended by local rancher Dickson White. In gratitude for helping White's son, the noted local benefactor paid Murchison's tuition at a police training academy in California.

The plot was definitely thickening.

* * * * *

I spent the rest of the day reading books about Steens Mountain and the nearby Alvord Desert. Two of them were by E. R. Jackman, a longtime Oregon Extension Service agent, who had a special interest in southeastern Oregon.

"Most mountains," he wrote, "such as individual peaks in the Cascades, Rockies, or Appalachians, are parts of a long chain. Not so Steens Mountain, for it stands alone in the desert. It is one of Oregon's famous 'fault mountains,' as the geologists call them." Unlike these other mountain ranges, Steens Mountain is made of lava coming up from below Earth's crust. This is different from the lighter sandstone or limestone of the Rockies. Each fault mountain is what is called a huge up-thrust block. This means that it has a gradual incline from the west—twenty-three miles from its base to the top—but only three miles from the top to the eastern flat plain below. As a result, the Steens Mountain has no foothills. Nor is it a range of mountains, hence its name: Steens *Mountain*, with no S.

That explained what I had already seen: the gradual incline up a straight road with few twists and turns like in the mountains I was used to. From all I had heard about it, the view from the top was breathtaking, with the Alvord Desert below to the east and a lot of interesting canyons on either side of the main road on the way up.

Somehow, by myself or with the help of others, I would explore as much of the territory in this wild and dangerous part of Oregon as I could over the next few weeks. My goal was a simple one: find Mike Tateman or, more likely, the remains of Mike Tateman.

I continued to be troubled by Margot's seeming inability to grieve. She hadn't cried in my presence or even choked up when she talked about the disappearance of her husband. In a search engine, I typed in "Coping with grief after a sudden death" and found at least a partial answer. "Because of the sudden nature of the death," stated one entry, "you may experience an unexpected sequence of feelings. Specifically, you may have a delayed grief reaction, resulting from the difficulty of being able to initially comprehend the events or the meaning of the death."

CHAPTER 19

AFTER SPENDING THE MORNING PAYING BILLS and cleaning my house in Newport, I drove to Salem in another rental car. I figured I'd be gone for at least two weeks, so I packed enough clothes for that length of time.

Lorenzo had finished his legal work for the day when I walked in the door to his building.

"Lock the front door," he yelled from his office in the back. I twisted the dead bolt lock into place and walked down the familiar hall.

"You know, Lorenzo," I said, as I stepped into his office, "this place could use a good coat of paint. Why don't you have a few of these guys you save from deportation grab some brushes?"

"You know, Tom, that's a good idea. Why didn't I think of that?" he said smiling.

He got up from his desk and walked around to embrace me. We patted each other on the back before I sat down. Then he poured two cups of coffee and handed me one of the mugs.

"Okay, so tell me what you found over there in the wilds of eastern Oregon. At least you weren't strung up by your liberal neck. How'd you get along among the rednecks?"

I filled him in on details about my various unpleasant encounters—with the sheriff and his deputy. I also mentioned what my student was researching and what he had found out so far about the two men and both Whites. I also recounted the odd conversation I had had with Dickson White.

"Dickson White," he said when he heard the name. "Seems like I filed a suit against him a few years back for exploiting the migrant workers he hired for his ranch." He thought for a moment and then pointed to his head. "Bingo. I do still have a mind! We won that suit, and he had to not only pay back wages but also clean up the bunkhouse he forced the workers to live in. I think he'd even charged them rent for a shithole that didn't even have indoor plumbing. Seems like one of the guys even got bit by a rat when he went to the outhouse at night."

He smiled at the memory of what had happened next. "Oh yeah, we fixed Mr. Dickson White pretty good. He drove up to the courthouse in Bend every day in a bright yellow Hummer, but we had to get a change of venue; he knew so many people in the county over there that we were worried they'd side with him against the workers. He was not very happy when he lost. It's probably rare for him to lose at anything he does."

"I'll bet he hated to be beaten by a Hispanic—I mean, you," I said. "He likes to intimidate people, not meet them in court as equals. Let me guess—you were in your best three-piece, pin-striped suit with a sparkling white shirt and matching tie and pocket handkerchief."

"How'd you know?" He laughed. "I like to look my best when I'm in court. I don't think that jeans and a blue work shirt really cut it with jurors."

"Did any of the ladies on the jury swoon when you did your best Antonio Banderas imitation?"

"*Si, señor*," he said with a big grin.

"So that lets you out to do undercover work for me in the Steens," I said, shaking my head.

"Maybe not. After you were here last time, I called an old college buddy from that area, Jesus Arriaga. He goes by Jason now. He's Basque and his family has raised sheep for over 100 years. He lives in San Francisco now but keeps in close touch with his mom and brother. The father died a few years ago, but his family still runs sheep on rangeland somewhere out near the Steens. I asked him to see if his brother knew of any *gringo* who had disappeared over there. He said he'd get back to me. He owes me. A couple of years ago, I got his younger brother off on a drug charge. Not sure the treatment facility I got him into really cured him, but at least he didn't shame his mother by going to jail."

"That kind of help is what we need," I said. "You think he'd talk to me?"

"Yeah, or maybe I'll take a road trip and see him myself. He said he'd be spending some time on the ranch later in May. Besides, he likes me—a lot."

"In the Biblical sense?" I laughed. "I take it he's gay."

Lorenzo nodded. "That's why he doesn't live on the home ranch in southeast Oregon. The men over there would tear him limb from limb if they knew—cowboys are beyond homophobic. I do like the guy but strictly as a friend. I'll look into this some more and let you know if he or his brother can help us."

The two of us worked out a system for keeping in touch and discussed how he thought we should proceed from here. He didn't say anything about his investigator, Trina Hutchins, so I didn't mention her. Maybe he had her on another assignment. I had my doubts anyway as to how she would fit in and be able to do her job over there, where African Americans were as rare as college professors trying to find lost people.

We left his office and drove to his house. After an excellent dinner prepared by his housekeeper, I went to bed early so I would be rested for my long drive.

CHAPTER 20

ON THE DRIVE TO FRENCHGLEN, I debated about how I would accomplish my task. Given the small population of the area, a stranger like me would stand out. I had already posed as a tourist just passing through. The longer I hung around, the more people would wonder why I was really there. That would include the sheriff, who had met me and would be suspicious about why I had returned.

I saw no other way than to tell the truth from the start and see if that yielded some results. I needed to find out if Mike Tateman was still alive—which I doubted—and if not to find his body so that Margot could bury him and mourn properly. Then, for her sake and Ned's, I had to figure out how he had died.

I planned to go to the sheriff and ask about his investigation and then follow as many leads as I could turn up, with or without his help. My former student, Jeff Walls, would help me with his knowledge of the area and the contacts he had from years of living in the area. Lorenzo would find out what he could from his friend, the Basque guy, and keep me out of legal trouble.

At 7:15 p.m., I pulled up in front of the *Burns Beacon* office. I had phoned Jeff about an hour before that, so he was waiting for me. He walked down the steps of the building.

"Let's go on over to the Cattlemen's and have some dinner," he said, shaking my hand. "I'm starved."

We made the short walk to the café and sat down in a booth at the rear.

"Would you like coffee?" This waitress was younger than the one who had served us lunch a few weeks ago.

"Sure, Penny," smiled Jeff. "How ya doin' tonight?"

She blushed as she filled his cup. "I'm good, thanks." Turning to me, she asked, "You, sir?"

"Please."

She poured coffee in my cup and handed us two of those menus with the selections encased in plastic and the edges held by small black tabs. "The special tonight is lamb chops with potatoes and gravy."

"Thanks. Give us a minute," said Jeff.

"I think Penny likes you," I said.

"Well, maybe, but I try to keep away from girls like that. Sweet but mixed up. We went to high school together, and she was knocked up by a football player in our senior year and had to leave school to care for her kid. The father is a real jerk—Junior White, the guy we talked about when you were here before, and I sent you some material on."

"I remember. Sounds like a real winner."

"Yeah. White senior put poor Penny through hell, trying to prove the kid wasn't his son's so he wouldn't have to pay his worthless son's child support. She got so upset that she quit trying to get anything. She's raising the kid with the help of her parents. Ricky's about six now. He's got some health problems, maybe borderline autism and bad asthma, and he's real hyperactive. She'd like to put him in a special school in the valley but can't afford it. She talks about her problems with anyone who will listen. I'm sympathetic, but . . ." He put down his menu. "What looks good to you? I'm having the lamb chops. You know you're in sheep country, Tom. It'd be fresh."

"I've never been a fan of lamb," I said. "As I'm taking the first bite, I can't help but think of those cute little creatures that were sacrificed to give people like you something to bite into."

Penny stood at the table, pen and pad at the ready.

"I'll have that great old staple of country diners everywhere: chicken fried steak," I told her.

"You don't have any sympathy for cows, Tom?" Jeff smiled and looked up at Penny. "This tab's for me, and I'm forgetting my manners. Penny Brando, this is my old professor from college, Thomas Martindale."

"Hello. It is great to meet you." We shook hands.

"I'm impressed. It isn't every day that we get a real college professor here in Burns," Penny replied and walked away.

"It never ceases to amaze me that people in the real world are so impressed with college professors. You and I know that many of them are nothing special, even though they think they are."

"You're pretty sour on academe, aren't you?" said Jeff.

"Yeah, I guess, but I still love working with students and helping them move out into their careers."

"Like me," he said. "You know, I owe you a lot. If it wasn't for you, I'd be working in the woods or punching cattle."

"Nonsense," I said. "A smart kid like you is born with ability. Somehow, it's in your genes. The ability to write can't really be taught. It's almost a mysterious process that I can't explain. You can either do it innately or you can't. What I gave you was the opportunity—in class and during internships—to bring that out. I gave you the platform on which to perform."

Our salads arrived and I put a lot of Thousand Island dressing on mine, which did not have all the weird, weed-like greens the fancy places foist on diners. "I love iceberg lettuce," I said, taking my first bite.

During the course of our supper, Jeff told me that he had found out that Clay Murchison, the sheriff's nephew, had been disciplined several times since he joined the force. All of the infractions involved his being overly aggressive with the motorists he stopped for speeding. Each time, because of the sheriff's intervention, Clay was allowed to return to work.

"I wonder how the other deputies feel about that." I finished my steak and pushed the plate away.

"Most of them don't have the balls to go up against the sheriff, with one exception: Hank French. He's a descendant of Pete French, the first cattleman in this area. The town's named after him; Hank's like royalty for that reason. Even the sheriff doesn't want to tangle with him. Not sure why he doesn't run for sheriff. Maybe he's biding his time. I'll introduce you, and maybe he can help you find Mr. Tateman."

"Good idea. I think I should go through the sheriff first, and then follow up with French or anybody else who might help me after that. I don't expect Sheriff Murchison to lift a finger to help me, but I'd at least like to know if he's conducting an investigation."

"If he is," said Jeff, "it's pretty much undercover. No one knows about it and that doesn't happen in a place like this where everyone knows everything. If he and his men were looking for someone, people around here would offer to help. And I'd hear about it. I haven't heard a thing."

We finished our meals and I looked at my watch.

"I'd better find a room for the night. I didn't make any reservations."

"Why don't you stay with me?" said Jeff. "I'm living in my family's old farmhouse just outside of town. It's a great old house, built in the 1880s. I've done a lot of improvements I'd like you to see. I rattle around in it and would like your company. You'd have your own room and bath. I'll give you a key, and you can come and go anytime you want to. Hell, I spend most of my time at the newspaper, so I'm not even home much. But, it's not a bachelor pig sty. I've got a cleaning lady who cleans once a week and even prepares meals in advance for me."

"I'm convinced, Jeff. It sounds great. You live better than I do."

We both laughed and walked to the front, where he paid the check.

"Great to see you, Penny. How's your son doing?" asked Jeff.

Penny's face fell, as she put the money in the cash register and his tip in her pocket. "Oh, you know Ricky. He's not an easy kid to manage. He's sick a lot and has trouble in school. I wish I could send him to the valley to get some real help. I worry, too, that he'll grow up without a proper role model. His daddy's sure never been that."

Jeff looked nervous at what she was saying. "Well, gotta go. Take care."

We stepped outside and walked toward the newspaper office.

"Now that was a proposal if I ever heard one," I commented.

"Don't you think I don't know it," he said, "but that would be the end of me in more ways than one. Penny's a sweet girl but she made her bed, so to speak, and now she's got to lie in it."

"Cruel, but true."

I waited on the porch of the office while Jeff went back in to grab his briefcase and turn off the lights. As we rounded the building to reach our cars, I noticed a sheriff's patrol car parked on the adjacent street. It was so dark, however, that I couldn't tell who was behind the wheel.

CHAPTER 21

THE QUIET OF THE HIGH DESERT put me right to sleep that night, and I didn't wake up until after eight the next morning, which was late for me. I showered and dressed and went downstairs. As I expected, Jeff had already left for the newspaper office.

A pot of coffee and a plate of cinnamon rolls were sitting on the counter in the kitchen. While I had breakfast, I checked for messages on my home phone. There was only one, from Margot Tateman: "Sorry I've been so out of reach. Good luck with your investigation. Thanks for doing this for me, Tom. Bye for now." She sounded tired, and her voice was so soft I could barely hear it.

After washing the dishes, I checked the local phone book for the sheriff's number, then dialed it.

"Sheriff Murchison's office."

"I was calling to make an appointment to see the sheriff, today if possible."

"If this is an emergency, you need to call 9-1-1."

"No, I'm not calling for that. I want to talk to him about a case, or at least I think it's a case."

"Perhaps you need to talk to one of our detectives. I can transfer you."

This was a lot harder than I expected. "No, I need to talk to the sheriff. The husband of a friend of mine has disappeared on Steens Mountain, and I have come here to look into the situation for her."

"I can transfer you to the person who handles missing persons. Just hang on." She put me on hold for a moment, then returned to the line. "Sir, that person is not picking up."

"Wait, wait. Please, just let me come in and talk to the sheriff. He knows about the case. Just tell him it's about Michael Tateman. The sheriff has talked to his wife. She's the reason I am here," I said.

"And her name is?"

"Margot Tateman."

"Is that M A R G O or M A R G O T?"

"Yes, with a T."

"And what is your name, sir?"

"Tom Martindale."

"Is that M A R T I N G A L E?"

"No, it's Martin-dale, with a D. No G."

"Let me see about the sheriff's schedule. He's a very busy man."

"I'm sure he is."

"I can fit you in a week from today."

"I'm only here for a few days. Any chance for some time today—like, in fifteen minutes?"

I could tell that she had put her hand over the mouthpiece of the phone. She was talking to someone, but I couldn't hear what was being said. After a moment, she came back to me. "You're in luck. The sheriff just walked in, and he said to come right over. Do you know where we're located?"

She gave me directions, and I thanked her and hung up.

* * * * *

The receptionist at the sheriff's office led me through a door behind her desk and into a large room filled with desks where a number of deputies were either working on computers or standing around with coffee cups in their hands. One of them was Clay Murchison. I nodded at him as we passed; he whispered something to the guy standing with him, and they both laughed.

The sheriff barely looked up from the papers he was reading as I walked in the door.

"Sheriff, this is your ten o'clock, Mr. Martingale."

It took another few minutes for the sheriff to acknowledge either of us.

"Okay, Donna," the sheriff finally said to the receptionist. Then turning to me, he said, "Sit, sit." He motioned me to a chair and took several sips from a large cup.

Even though I had already had my quota of coffee for the day, he didn't know that. It seemed the height of rudeness that he didn't offer me something to drink.

I decided not to wait for him to talk. "Hello, sheriff. Thanks for seeing me on such short notice. Not sure if you remember that . . ."

"I know, I know. You were with Jeff Walls in the Cattlemen's a couple of weeks ago. You're his professor or some bullshit like that."

"Yes, that's right. I wondered if . . ."

"So, what brings you back to our fair city again so soon? Usually people like you from the valley can only stand to be with us hicks . . . is it 'us' hicks or 'we' hicks?"

"I'm not sure, and it doesn't really matter."

"It matters to me when people think I'm ignorant because I make mistakes in the way I speak." The sheriff was serious.

I get very impatient with people who are always fretting about the way other people speak, correcting their grammar when it really doesn't make any difference. Everyday speech is colloquial and doesn't always have to be by the book.

"I'd have said 'us' hicks, I guess."

"Okay, glad to have that out of the way. Now, what's this case all about? You say a woman named Margot is missing. You related to her? Is she your girlfriend?"

This was turning into more of a hassle than I expected, less a conspiracy than a comedy of errors.

"Let me start at the beginning. An old friend from high school, Margot Tateman, called me a few weeks ago to say that her husband, Michael Tateman, a Portland attorney, was missing somewhere out here. He went hiking on Steens Mountain last month and has not been heard from since. You and she talked. In fact, you called her to tell her that he was missing, and she and her son came over here to talk to you about what happened."

The sheriff tapped his head as if that would allow him to remember. "Oh yeah, it's coming back to me. They wanted to know if we were looking for him. She wanted all kinds of search parties organized and planes flying over the area. I felt she didn't think I knew what I was doing. I've been in law enforcement all my working life, so I pretty damn well know how to look for people. I don't need some fancy rich lady from Portland to come over here and get all high-hat with me and tell me how to do my job."

Something in Margot's attitude had really set Murchison off, but I knew she was not like that. Any impression he had to the contrary was wrong.

"Sheriff Murchison, I've known Margot for years. She is a good person, but she is also someone who is beside herself with grief. Her husband of many years is missing, and she is frantic to find him or find out what happened to him. She can't handle his business affairs. She can't bury him and have a funeral. She is stuck on square one. I'm sure she didn't mean to imply that you weren't doing your best."

"All that talk about bringing in the FBI. I don't need the FBI to big-foot around and muck up my investigation."

Bingo. That was the key to his attitude. Margot had mentioned the FBI, and it had really set Murchison off.

"I don't know anything about jurisdictions, and I doubt Margot does either," I said. "She's just seen too many TV shows where the FBI comes in and saves the day."

"That'll be the day," he scoffed. "They usually don't know their asses from a hole in the ground. They come in with their white shirts and narrow ties and short haircuts and start flashin' their badges. It scares people."

"Let's put that thought to rest and forget the FBI," I said, trying to soothe him. "I'm just wondering if you did conduct a search and if you found anything." I braced for another outburst. It came after he finished his coffee.

"I am responsible for this whole goddamned county. It's one of the largest in the state. Did you know that? I haven't got enough deputies. Hell, I don't even have enough patrol cars for them. We do what we can with what we've got. So when a guy from outside turns up missing, we take a slow approach. I don't have the resources to do the big search she was talking about. Who the hell knows, maybe he's run off with his secretary. Maybe he's taking an unexpected trip overseas. Maybe he's faking the whole thing to collect some insurance or access an offshore bank account. How the hell do I know?"

But you should at least go through the motions of finding out, I thought but did not say.

"I've taken enough of your time," I said, glancing at my watch. "Bottom line here is that your preliminary search has not turned up anything. Am I right? I'm not passing judgment, just asking so I can tell Margot."

Murchison stood up.

"The case file is open, and I will proceed when I have something to go on."

"Is anyone handling the case full-time?"

"Not full-time. I've got one of my deputies keeping up on developments when there are any developments. You saw him when we met in the café. His name is Clay. He's my nephew. A little green and hot-headed, but he's on his way to becoming a fine law enforcement officer."

CHAPTER 22

THERE WERE MORE CARS parked in front of the Frenchglen Hotel than when I had been there the month before. I walked up the steps and into the screened porch without looking closely at the people sitting there.

"As I live and breathe," said a voice, "it's Tom Martindale."

"By golly, I do believe it is," said another.

I turned to see Herb and Sue Grover, who were sitting with another woman drinking ice tea.

"Herb and Sue. Great to see you again. I didn't expect to see the two of you either. Don't tell me, let me guess. It's a great time for birders out here."

"You can say that again, by golly," said Herb. "You checkin' in?"

"No, I'm staying in Burns with a friend."

"Tom, I want you to meet one of our dearest friends and fellow birder, Catherine Rickbone," said Sue.

A tall, slim woman with gray hair cut in a very stylish way stood up and extended her hand. "You're the professor the Grovers told me about. I'm glad to meet you."

"Me as well. You're all going to climb the mountain in search of birds for your list?"

"You betcha," said Herb. "Can't wait. We're going first thing in the morning."

Just then, I caught sight of a sheriff patrol car slowing down outside; it did not stop. Deputy Clay was on the job, no doubt. I had an idea.

"Would you guys mind some company? I've always wanted to look for birds with people who know what they are. I don't know a robin from a seagull, but I'd like to learn."

This would be a perfect way to throw both Murchisons off track. I could hide in plain sight with the Grovers and Ms. Rickbone.

"By golly, we'd love to have you with us! Right ladies?"

The two nodded enthusiastically.

"Be here at 6 a.m.—Mr. Bates has agreed to fix us some breakfast and lunch to go." He leaned over to me. "For some extra money, I'll just have him add enough for you."

"That will be great. I'll see you in the morning. And thanks."

"You're very welcome, by golly."

* * * * *

In George Gershwin's musical *Crazy for You*, two British tourists show up in the fictional town of Deadrock, Nevada, and are portrayed as figures of fun. They are dressed in khaki shorts, bush jackets, and pith helmets. Although guidebook writers, they have always embodied for me the stereotypical innocents who stumble into situations more complicated than they expected. To add to the merriment, they have accents that are at times indecipherable. I'm afraid I'm influenced by that stereotype now.

The Grovers and Ms. Rickbone were similarly attired when we met on the screen porch just before 6 a.m. While I wore jeans, a blue work shirt, and a fleece jacket, all three of them were visions in khaki. Each of them carried two of something I wished I had: binoculars.

"You can never have too many binoculars, by golly," said Herb, as he handed me one of his. "You can't see a lot of the little guys we are looking for without them."

"Looks like it will be a gorgeous day," said Sue, gesturing toward the east where the sun was rising in blinding glory of yellow against the clear blue sky.

"It will be a good day to be outside," said Ms. Rickbone.

"Good morning, Ms. Rickbone. Are you as committed to bird watching as the Grovers?" I asked.

"Please call me Catherine, Tom. Yes, I've been looking for bird species all over the world for years."

"Her life list's got a lot more entries than ours, by golly," said Herb.

The door opened and Mr. Bates handed each of us a paper bag and also sandwich bags with what looked like egg and bacon sandwiches. "Here's a thermos of coffee, too," he said.

Herb slipped some money into his shirt pocket. "Thank you, my friend," he said.

"Yes, thank you," the rest of us said in unison.

I walked up to Herb. "Here, take some money. You shouldn't have to pay for this."

"It hardly cost a thing. It's our pleasure to have you with us, by golly."

"I'm looking forward to the day," I replied. And I really was, despite the fact that my day of birding was really an unobtrusive way to get up on the mountain. Even though the sheriff and his deputy knew I was here, they might be slightly thrown off by the sight of me looking at birds through binoculars.

We walked to the Grovers' car, a big SUV. I was glad he was driving because I did not want to damage my rental car with flying gravel.

"Sit up front with me," said Herb, "so you can see better. The ladies don't mind sitting in the back, right sweetie?"

"Not at all," said the two from the rear.

We turned right onto Highway 205 and, after less than a mile, turned left onto the road up the mountain.

Herb turned his head toward the backseat. "Want to read from that booklet I gave you this morning, sweetie?" he said.

Sue cleared her throat. "This is from a booklet Herb got from the Fish and Wildlife Service," she began.

"Louder, sweetie, by golly," said Herb. "We can't hear you over the engine noise and the bumps in the road."

She cleared her throat again and started over. This time her voice came through loud and clear. "I think the wildlife service excerpted some of the writings of E. R. Jackman. Are you familiar with him, Tom?"

"Yes, I am."

"Here goes. 'Since its establishment in 1908, biologists and other skilled observers at the Malheur National Wildlife Refuge have been listing bird species. They have seen 227 species common to the area and have noted another 21 that are relatively rare or accidental visitors, making a total of 248.' Isn't that remarkable?"

"Amazing," I said. "I had no idea."

"That's enough of that," said Herb. "I just wanted to give you an idea of what we might see today. I say 'might' because you never know which of those little fellas will show up on any given day. Also, that booklet is about the Malheur National Wildlife Refuge, which is some miles north of here. We'll go there tomorrow, but I always like to start up on the mountain to see all the wonderful views. It's a unique place, by golly. You won't equal it anywhere."

We drove in silence for the next fifteen minutes, with Herb concentrating on avoiding the many potholes in the road, and the rest of us looking out the windows. Patches of snow dotted the landscape, and wildflowers were beginning to stick their heads up where the snow wasn't too deep.

At one point, Herb slammed on the brakes and jumped out of the car, as if he had been stung by a bee. He ran toward a grove of trees on the left and stopped, scanning the tree line with his binoculars. I got out and looked over the car in the same direction. While I saw only a slight movement in the limbs near the top, Herb had better luck.

"IT'S A GREAT BLUE HERON," he shouted. "WHAT A GREAT WAY TO START THE DAY!"

I got back inside the car.

"Herb loves blue herons," explained Sue.

"Can you add it to your list?" I asked.

"No, we've seen them many times."

"I've seen many before, but I'm going to add them to my count for this area," said Catherine.

"Whew!" said Herb, as he got back into the car, breathless but happy. "I think I just saw both a Golden Eagle way up in the air and an American Kestrel, by golly. Most of these birds hang out around the large bodies of water over in the refuge, but some of them fly over here from time to time. The small lakes and streams in these gorges attract them. With all the species of birds in this area, I'm really in hog heaven when I'm here—or should I say 'bird' heaven?" Herb broke into gales of laughter at his little joke.

"Oh, Herb," said Sue. "You're really something else!"

We stopped several more times on the way up to the top to view a Black Rosy-Finch and a Greater Sage-Grouse. As Herb drove, the three of them chatted away about birds they had seen in their long years as bird watchers. I smiled and nodded but soon tuned out all their talk of wild geese and ducks, hawks, trumpeter swans, horned owls, and turkey vultures.

"Penny for your thoughts, Tom, by golly," said Herb.

"I was just taking in all this beauty. I was also thinking that some of those bird names reminded me of the academic world, especially turkey vultures!"

They all laughed at my little joke, which gave me a nice recovery from my inattention to them.

It took over an hour to reach the summit of the mountain. As we got out of the car, I glimpsed two large black birds swooping down from a tree and heading north.

"What are those?"

"Oh, those are buzzards," said Herb. "They usually roost on a lookout tower at the P Ranch north of here. They must have gotten off course this morning."

In any portent of death and danger that I had ever heard of, buzzards made the top of the list. I shuddered as I watched them fly out of sight.

I walked to the edge to get a better view. While the west side of the mountain was on a gradual incline, the east side was abrupt and steep. Anyone dumb enough to step too close would fall thousands of feet to certain death on the desert floor below. Mike Tateman crossed my mind. If he had fallen from here, there wouldn't be anything much left of him after he hit the ground. I made a mental note to include the area of the Alvord Desert just below in my later search.

From here, the view was spectacular—to Idaho and beyond. The predominant color was gray-black, like lava. Indeed, that is what made the mountain thousands of years ago. The contrast with the sandy desert below was distinct. Added to this colorful mix were the white clouds that seemed to hang over us, not in a threatening way as if they were hiding thunder and lightning, but as a means to shift the color as their moving shadows covered the ground.

Catherine walked up next to me. "This is really something!" she said. "I have traveled to many places but this has to be one of the most beautiful."

"I agree," I said. "It really takes your breath away, trite as that sounds. I can't put into words the grandeur of this place."

Herb and Sue walked up to us and stood quietly.

"This mountain is the focal point for several gorges," said Herb. He put on his glasses and read from a book. "Here's what E. R. Jackman said about these gorges. I think it puts it all into perspective, now that we're here in the middle of them. 'Each of these gorges cut through and exposed the numerous lava flows, as the layers of a cake are exposed when a slice is removed. The color shown on the rims is due to lichens.' Lichens are that fungus that grows on rocks and trees," he said. "By golly, you can see it if you look close."

The four of us split up and walked to different points of the escarpment. Catherine kept scanning the sky for birds. Sue bent down to look for wildflowers. Herb was reading the manual for his camera. I walked to a point where I had a side view of the steep cliffs. A narrow ledge ran along the wall, and I stepped up on it and started walking. The view from this higher point was even more breathtaking than below—the colors were more vivid, and I could see even farther. I felt close to the clouds.

Halfway across to what looked like a dead end where a huge rock stopped all passage, I leaned back against the wall and gazed outward once more. At one point, I glanced at the lava wall next to me to examine the rock and the lichen more closely. Something metallic caught my eye. It was out of place in this natural setting. I reached down and picked it up: an Indian head penny, old and no longer in use, but as bright and shiny as the day it was minted.

* * * * *

"You were taking kind of a chance back there, by golly," said Herb, as we drove to another viewpoint. "If you'd fallen, we'd be picking up the pieces in the Alvord Desert."

"Yeah, I guess I got carried away with that great view." I hadn't mentioned the penny, whose meaning I had yet to figure out. If Mike Tateman carried the old penny as some kind of good luck charm, it was a real find. If not, I had found my own lucky piece.

Herb stopped the car. "Let's walk along the path over there to get to where we can see into Kiger Gorge."

We all climbed out of the car and followed him down a rocky and uneven path. For a big man, Herb was quite agile.

"Be careful, by golly," he said over his shoulder. "It gets kind of slippery along here."

After a few hundred yards we came to the end of this escarpment, although there was no sheer drop-off like there was on the other side. A gradual decline led into the gorge, and the rough pathway seemed to make a turn to the left. To get ready for the trip, I had read about the mountain and learned that the unusual shape—the gradual incline up the west side and the sheer drop on the east side—was caused by glaciers that dug trenches about a half-mile deep through layers of hard basalt. This resulted in four glacial cuts, the gorges of the Steens: Kiger, Little Blitzen, Big Indian, and Wildhorse. Massive internal pressures forced the east edge upward, resulting in a thirty-mile-long fault-block mountain (the largest in the northern Great Basin) with the rugged east face that rises above the Alvord Desert.

"It looks like an easy stroll, and I've known a few guys who hike down there, but it's pretty steep on the way back up," said Herb. "Supposed to be a herd of wild horses living there, purebred mustangs that are descended from the horses the Spanish conquistadors brought to North America. The BLM keeps them out of sight of the visitors so they won't be bothered. They also control the breeding of them, to keep the bloodlines pure I guess. They only allow a few of them to be adopted each year."

"I saw wild horses when I was here a few weeks ago," I said. "They were farther down the main road, next to a ranch."

"They're from a different herd, and the BLM holds auctions regularly to keep the number from getting out of hand," said Herb. "You see them in all colors, but the horses in Kiger Gorge look different. They have a stripe down their backs just like zebras, and their manes are long and bicolored. Their ears are kind of hooked and tipped with black. They've also got stripes on their legs."

"How do they keep them separate?" asked Catherine.

"Partly by watching them closely and partly because the horses shy away from human contact. It's like they want to be alone. I'm sure there are a few big stallions guarding the herd and keeping the mares and foals in line—stallions nobody would want to tangle with."

"Interesting," I said, absent-mindedly fingering the penny in my pocket.

* * * * *

It was late afternoon when we pulled into the parking lot of the hotel. A familiar-looking car was parked next to mine.

"Looks like we'll have company for dinner," said Sue.

We got out and walked up the steps to the screened porch, where a woman and a man sat drinking beer from bottles.

"Well, who do we have here?" said Herb, extending his hand.

"I'm Lorenzo Madrid and this is my wife, Trina Hutchins," said the dashingly handsome Hispanic man.

"Did anyone ever tell you that you look just like that movie actor, Antonio Banderas?" said Catherine, who seemed ready to swoon.

CHAPTER 23

I HID MY ASTONISHMENT at seeing Lorenzo and Trina by waiting to step forward until the others had introduced themselves. Given our task here, it would be better if no one knew our connection. I liked Herb, Sue, and Catherine, but they had a tendency to talk a lot. Under the old "loose lips sink ships" scenario of World War II, our connection had to be secret.

I could tell by the look in Lorenzo's eyes that he felt the same. Hopefully, the freewheeling Trina would follow his lead.

"Tom Martindale. Mr. and Mrs. Madrid, is it?"

"I prefer Ms. Hutchins," said Trina. "Mrs. Madrid sounds like a contestant in a Spanish beauty pageant."

We all laughed at her remark, which broke the proverbial ice. I shook hands with both of them.

"Well, by golly, I think we all need something to drink. Wine?" said Herb, looking at the three of us.

"White," said Sue.

"Me too," I added.

"Red for me," said Catherine.

"My wife and I will have another beer," said Lorenzo.

"I don't suppose they have Mexican brands," asked Trina, grimacing at the bottle in front of her. "I really never drink anything . . ."

"Whatever they have is fine," interrupted Lorenzo.

"I'll get the drinks and tell Mr. Bates that you'll be staying for dinner, Tom. Okay?" said Herb.

"Thank you."

"Oh, you're not staying in the hotel?" asked Lorenzo.

"No, I'm staying in Burns with a former student of mine. He runs the local newspaper and lives in a big farmhouse he inherited from his parents. I'm using the house as my base of operations, so to speak, but I intend to come back over here every day I'm in the area. I've stayed in this hotel before—you'll be very comfortable."

"Herb and I have been here a number of times, and we love it," said Sue. "It's kind of a pain to have to go down the hall to the bathroom, but you get used to it."

"I'm in one of the newer units in a separate building in the back," said Catherine. "It has an all-new and modern bathroom."

"At least we don't have to use an outhouse," said Trina.

Herb returned with the drinks on a tray. "Here we are, by golly," he said, as he handed each of us a glass. He drank heartily from a bottle of beer.

"Easy, dear," said Sue. "Remember your liver."

"So, I'd guess you're from the valley?" I asked.

"Salem," said Lorenzo.

"Portland," said Trina at the same time, and forgetting that they were supposed to be married. "I mean Portland *and* Salem. I live in Salem with Lorenzo, of course, but do some of my work in Portland. It's not that far."

"I teach law at Willamette University," said Lorenzo. That was technically correct because he had taught an evening class at the law school as pro bono work for several years. "Trina is a private investigator."

The other three looked at one another in astonishment. Most people had read about fictional private investigators or seen their exploits on television but few had ever met one.

"Now that is really something, by golly," said Herb.

"That must be fascinating," said Catherine.

"Isn't it dangerous?" asked Sue.

Trina finished her beer and put the bottle on the table. She was milking the moment for as long as she could. "Not really. I don't have to skulk around in a trench coat or carry a gun in my garter belt. I don't have to use a camera with a long lens to take pictures of a guy in bed with his mistress. These days, a lot of what I do is done on the Internet, searching records for business and personal stuff. It's pretty tame. I've done some of that other stuff in the past but not anymore."

"Trina and I agreed when we got married that she'd refuse those kinds of jobs," said Lorenzo, easily slipping into the role of the caring husband. "It's much too dangerous, right honey?"

Trina Hutchins was the last woman who would want to be called "honey," but she was playing her own role—that of the dutiful wife.

"Yes, baby doll, you got it. I need to keep myself safe for you." She batted her eyes and squeezed his arm.

"Well, by golly, I wonder if dinner's about ready," said Herb, clearly nervous at this public sign of affection. "I'll go in and see."

Lorenzo and I exchanged glances.

"So, what do you do, Mr. Martin, was it?" he asked.

"Martindale. I'm a college professor and an author."

"Do tell," said Lorenzo. "What do you teach, and what do you write about?"

* * * * *

After a delicious dinner of the chef's special meatloaf, we sat around the table and talked for about an hour. Herb, Sue, and Catherine were nice people and Lorenzo, Trina, and I relaxed into an easy banter with them.

As we were finishing dessert, Clay Murchison, his cowboy friend Marty, and his fiancée Lurlene, walked in. The cowboy and his girl sat down at the same table as before, but Clay, who was not in uniform, could not resist making trouble. He walked over to our table and just stood there.

"Good evening, deputy. How are you tonight?" I said to him.

"So, what do we have here?" he said in a haughty way. He was slurring his words and smelled of liquor.

I shook my head at Lorenzo and stood up. "We're having dinner with our friends," I said. "Why don't you go and enjoy a nice dinner with your friends over there."

"You don't order me around, Mr. Big Shot Professor. I am the law around here."

By this time, both Marty and Lurlene had walked over to stand on either side of Clay.

"Come on, buddy," said Marty softly. "Come on over, and we'll get some of that meatloaf you love." He was using the same tone you would use with a child who was misbehaving.

"I don't want to sit down," said Clay. "I want to get to the bottom of what's going on here. Let me get this straight. We've got four white people—two fat, two regular size—sitting with a brown guy, and then there's this black chick."

Lorenzo stood up. I leaned close. "Don't go too far. He's the sheriff's nephew."

"That *chick,* as you call her, happens to be my wife," said Lorenzo, moving closer to Clay. "Whew. You've had too much to drink, *amigo.* You don't smell very good."

That remark enraged Clay and he swung his arm toward Lorenzo but didn't connect because Marty grabbed him and pulled him back.

"LEAVE ME BE," he yelled. "I NEED TO TEACH THIS BEANER A LESSON! AND HIS LITTLE NIGGER WIFE TOO!"

I pushed Lorenzo away from Clay and grabbed his arm. "Don't do what you have every right to do, or you'll wind up in a jail that probably looks like one you'd find in the deep South in the 1950s," I whispered. "And the sheriff might throw away the key."

Lorenzo dropped his arms and sat down. As Marty and Lurlene pulled Clay away, Trina moved her foot slightly so that it caught Clay's boot. Already off balance because of being dragged away, he fell flat on his face. He didn't seem to grasp what had happened at first, as he struggled to his feet with a bewildered look on his face. Trina winked at the rest of us and went back to eating her apple pie.

Marty jammed Clay's hat on his head and pushed him out the door. Lurlene walked over to our table.

"I am so sorry. My brother can't hold his liquor very well," she said, sadly. "He gets all crazy when he has too much to drink. I am so sorry."

"Not your fault, honey," said Trina, squeezing Lurlene's hand. "I look at stuff like that in a 'sticks and stones' way."

"Thanks for being so nice. You all have a nice night. Okay?"

Once again, Clay Murchison had ruined an evening for us at the Frenchglen Hotel.

"I thought you only read about guys like that in Gothic novels about the South before the Civil Rights Act was passed," I said, shaking my head. "He's a real jerk."

"No, I think he qualifies as a real asshole," said Catherine.

We all gasped at hearing such a word come out of the mouth of such a genteel lady.

"Well, sometimes even **I** have to resort to language that fits the occasion!"

The five of us laughed for a long time and then broke into applause.

"That's really what I meant, but I didn't think I should say it in front of you ladies," I said.

"Honey, you can't even imagine the bad words I've heard in my life," said Trina, shaking her head. "Some of them are so bad that I blush even when I think of them!"

We sat and talked for another hour. Finally, Mr. Bates cleared his throat and looked pointedly at his watch. He wanted to lock up.

"I've got to be getting back to town," I said with a yawn. I still thought it best to keep my friendship with Lorenzo and Trina from the others, and I knew we'd be in touch tomorrow.

We all shook hands and I agreed to return for dinner tomorrow night, after pleading that I had other things to do in town during the day.

I drove back to town without incident. Luckily, Deputy Clay was too drunk to follow me and pull me over on some trumped-up charge.

Jeff was still up when I walked in the door.

"I thought you'd be dead to the world by now," I said, sitting down in a chair next to the couch.

"I'm finishing up some editorials for this week's paper," he said. "Deadline's tomorrow."

"Do you like being the conscience of the town?"

"Not sure I'm that, but I do take care to have my facts straight and not just spout off for the sake of spouting off."

"I imagine your readers pay more attention to you because you're a local boy. I mean, it would be hard for an outsider to come in and tell them what to do."

"Yeah," he smiled ruefully. "It could happen, but it might take twenty years."

I told Jeff about the trip up the mountain, the unexpected arrival of Lorenzo and Trina, and the unpleasant encounter with Clay Murchison.

"Clay's a real jerk most of the time. And he's been in all that trouble for being overly aggressive that I already told you about." Jeff said.

My cell phone rang.

"Tom, it's Lorenzo."

"Anyone ever tell you that you sound like that movie star, let's see, I can't remember his name. . . ."

"Rudolph Valentino?" he said, with a laugh.

"Yeah, that's it!"

"How'd you get a call through without a cell tower?"

"I'm using the hotel phone," he said. "Sorry to drop in on you like that. It was Trina's idea. She likes the element of surprise."

"I was surprised all right, but no harm done. We need to meet and not talk about any of this stuff on the phone. Tomorrow morning. Just a minute. . . ." I turned to Jeff who had returned to his editing. "This is my attorney, Lorenzo Madrid. As I told you, he's here and we need to meet to talk about some stuff. Can we use your house?"

"Absolutely. I leave for work early, as you know, so act like this is your house. I've got plenty of coffee and there's eggs and bacon in the fridge."

"Great. Thanks." I put the phone back up to my ear. "Lorenzo, did you hear any of that? That's my friend Jeff Walls. I'm staying with him in Burns. We can hang out here all we want. More privacy and room to relax."

"Perfect," said Lorenzo. "Tell me how to find you."

"I'll put Jeff on the phone, and he can direct you."

"Mr. Madrid. Hi, I'm Jeff."

He gave Lorenzo the directions, and then I got back on the line and set our meeting time at ten.

"You'll probably want to have breakfast with Trina at the hotel. I don't think she should come with you. No offense to her, but she's too high profile for what we're trying to do here. You can blend in but the two of you together—a Hispanic man and a Black woman who are dressed like they just came from a photo shoot for *Vogue*—you'll stand out too much. Okay? I don't want to offend her."

"She'll understand. See you in the morning."

"Nice guy," said Jeff. "You know, he sounds like that Spanish movie actor. Let's see, what's his name?"

CHAPTER 24

LORENZO DROVE DOWN THE LONG DRIVEWAY to the farmhouse precisely at 10 a.m. I greeted him on the porch and we walked into the living room. I had cleared off a large library table and put two chairs on either side of it.

"Coffee?"

"No, I'm floating, and I'm also really full. The people at the Frenchglen know how to feed you. It's cholesterol city—pancakes and bacon and eggs, even cinnamon rolls. Delicious, but too much food!"

"Think of it as being on vacation. What did you do with Trina?"

"I convinced her to do some sightseeing with your friends, the birders. They were only too happy to take her under their wings, so to speak. I think they feel bad about what happened last night. She'll be fine. I probably shouldn't have brought her over here, but she really wanted to come."

"I hate it that she has to endure that kind of prejudice."

"She's tough, but I'm sure it gets to her. She's as qualified as any White person, but people react to her in a different way.

Beyond the outward prejudice, they might doubt her ability. I can see now that we're pretty high profile for this area. I have to admit that a Hispanic man and a Black woman will attract an extraordinary amount of attention. The nasty incident with the deputy proves that. It's hard to realize that rednecks like that still exist."

"You need to get out of the big cities more often, Lorenzo. Racial prejudice is alive and well in a lot of places in this country. You don't have to wear a white sheet with eyeholes cut into it to be a racist. I really don't think she can stay around here for very long. She'll attract too much attention. You're a different story. There are lots of Hispanics here, and you can blend in nicely as long as you shed your preppy outfit and put on a blue work shirt and jeans."

"You mean my wetback look?" He laughed.

"Precisely. Now, we need to talk about what I've found out so far and plan what you're going to do while you're here. You are going to do some poking around, I take it?"

"Yes. Remember my telling you about my friend from college, Jesus—or his Anglo name, Jason—Arriaga?"

"Yeah, the guy who has the hots for you."

"Yeah, that guy. You recall that I asked him to ask his family about Dickson White and your friend's missing husband. He called me two nights ago and said that he had found out some stuff and wanted to tell me about it in person. He's coming up here to visit his family, and I'm going to meet with him tonight."

"Good," I said. "At the family ranch?"

"No, at an old barn on their property. He doesn't want his brother to know he's meeting me. Not sure if he thinks his brother is involved or he's skittish about bringing another man there who he'd have to introduce to his mother."

"Sounds a bit fishy, Lorenzo. Are you sure he's not just trying to get you alone, to recapture some of that old magic?"

"That crossed my mind, so that's why I want you to go with me."

"Okay. That's a good idea but will he talk in front of me?"

"Yeah, I think he will because I already told him that you and I are an item. I hope you don't mind."

"It's okay. We need this to work."

Over the next few hours, we talked about all aspects of the case. I told him about my trip up Steens Mountain and finding the Indian head penny.

"Did your friend verify that it was her husband's good luck piece?"

"She hasn't gotten back to me yet. I'll be surprised if it wasn't."

Then, I put together a chart of where I thought we stood on Mike Tateman's disappearance.

MIKE TATEMAN
— drives to Steens;
 checks into Frenchglen Hotel;
 goes to Steens once, then returns;
 goes again and vanishes. What did he see?

DICKSON WHITE
— runs cattle on land around Steens, leery of strangers,
 close to sheriff?

SHERIFF MURCHISON
— seems to control area around Steens;
 probably protects White and son;
 keeps nephew on force despite problems on job;
 does not investigate Tateman's disappearance. Why?

JUNIOR WHITE

— in trouble all his life; gets Penny pregnant, won't pay child support.

DEPUTY CLAY

— does uncle's dirty work and is kept on force despite problems on job;
hot-headed, aggressive with motorists, etc.

MINOR PLAYERS

PENNY BRANDO

— girlfriend of Junior who has his child,
and whose father keeps him from paying child support; now bitter.

JEFF WALLS

— newspaper editor,
researching, knows major players.

JASON (JESUS) ARRIAGA

— Lorenzo's friend; some info on someone?

I sat back and pushed the paper over to Lorenzo. "Anything you can think of to add?"

"No, not at this point," he said, "but I just got here. You know the major players better than I do. I'd say we find out what Jason knows and then proceed from there. It seems like Dickson White is pretty protective of his land. Has he got something to hide? Did your friend's husband stumble onto something that was taking place on White's land or the nearby government land? Is his worthless son involved? Maybe Tateman found him doing something wrong, and White killed him to keep him quiet?" Lorenzo looked directly at me. "You do think he's dead, don't you?"

"Yeah. I'm afraid so. I don't say that to Margot directly, but we've got to face facts. His body is out there somewhere—or what's left. She probably realizes that too but can't really believe it until his remains are found. No need to be that blunt with her now. I guess it's our job to find out for sure so she can come to closure and bury him."

Lorenzo shook his head. "I can't think of anything worse. Scott was killed in front of me and as horrible as that was, at least I knew what happened to him."

He turned away with tears in his eyes.

* * * * *

After some debate, we decided that we would chance being seen in town together. Without Trina, the two of us could certainly have lunch. I called Jeff at his office, and he agreed to join us at the Cattlemen's Café at 1 p.m., after the noon lunch crowd had departed.

Jeff met us in front of the café and walked in with us. The older waitress, Dot, pointed to a booth in the back and handed us menus.

"What do you handsome guys want to drink?" she asked and winked at Lorenzo.

"Pepsi's all around?" I looked at them and they nodded.

Dot said, "I'll be back in a flash to see what you want to order," and went to get the drinks.

"Once again, you broke another heart, Lorenzo."

He blushed and Jeff smiled, even though he wasn't sure what we were talking about.

"Lorenzo here is pretty nice looking, wouldn't you agree?" I said to Jeff.

"Come off it, Tom. I get pretty sick of that subject." He looked at the menu.

"Okay, I know you do, but I have to explain this phenomenon to Jeff. Women think he's Antonio Banderas."

"That's who I thought you sounded like on the phone last night!" said Jeff. "I couldn't think of the name."

Lorenzo shook his head. "Even you are against me."

"Okay," I said. "Enough of that! I know it bothers you, and I won't bring it up again. But we should all have that kind of bother."

"You got *that* right," said Jeff.

Dot was back. "Okay, gents. What'll you have?"

"Chili burger for me," said Jeff.

"Same for me," I said.

"How's the special? The taco platter?" asked Lorenzo.

Dot turned and gestured toward the kitchen. "You see Diego in there? He's one of your people. He can make tacos in his sleep."

We all looked at the cook who had bent down so he could look at us in the pass-through window. He waved and we nodded in his direction.

"Sold," said Lorenzo with one of his killer smiles designed to melt the heart of any waitress.

"I think I'll change my order," I said.

We turned to Jeff.

"I'm sticking to my chili burger." He looked at the waitress. "Where's Penny? She's usually here at lunch."

"She's going through the wringer with that no-good ex-boyfriend of hers." She leaned in closer. "That good-for-nothing Junior White, who thinks he's God's gift to women."

Jeff shook his head in sympathy but didn't say any more. Dot walked away.

"So, Tom was your professor," said Lorenzo. "Did you learn anything from him?"

"Yes, I did. Don't tell him this, but I'd be tilling the soil or rounding up cattle if I hadn't gone to the university and taken one of his journalism classes. He changed my life."

"Wow, that's pretty high praise," said Lorenzo, smiling at me. "I can't believe it."

I ignored his kidding. "Jeff took classes from me in my early days of teaching when I was fresh from New York and rarin' to go. Later, I got pretty cynical and burned out. I look on those early days of teaching as the happiest time of my life."

"Well, it showed in your classes," said Jeff. "You were the only professor in the department who had had any experience. You wanted to convey that to us, and I'll always appreciate it."

"I could only tell you what I knew," I replied. "You had to have the talent to do something with it. You might get a job but then you have to perform.

"Jeff worked for the AP in different cities around the U.S. before buying this paper," I said to Lorenzo. "It's every newsperson's dream to buy your own paper."

"Do you like it?" asked Lorenzo.

"Most days, but it can be a pain in the ass sometimes and it's a lot of work. I do most of it myself, but I do have an ad salesman and a layout person."

"Can you really make a living from it?" I asked.

"Yeah, surprisingly so. I'm the only media outlet in town so I get all the advertising, and I keep my costs low. I also have a lock on giving the town the news. No one else covers this whole area, and many people who live out here are old-fashioned enough that they still like to read a newspaper once a week."

"Here you are, hon." Dot had returned with our food. She placed the plates in front of us.

"How can you carry all those plates without dropping at least one of them?" Lorenzo asked in his most sexy voice.

"Honey, it takes practice and, as the old saying goes, practice makes perfect." She winked at Lorenzo and walked away.

"We need to get down to business," I said, as I dug into my tacos, which were very good. "Jeff has found out a lot of background stuff on the sheriff and Dickson White. Very useful stuff. You can keep tabs on things here in town while we continue our investigation. I don't want to compromise you. We're leaving in a few days or weeks, but you live and make a living here."

"I can handle it," said Jeff. "Don't worry about me."

After a few more mouthfuls of taco, both Lorenzo and I toasted Diego with our Pepsis—he was again smiling at us in the pass-through window, which revealed a whole mouthful of gold crowns.

It was now 2 p.m., and we had the café to ourselves. The waitress had gone on a break and Diego was cleaning up his kitchen, so we could talk without worrying that someone would overhear us.

I filled Jeff in on what I had found out about the sheriff, the deputy, and Dickson White. I mentioned finding the Indian head penny and Lorenzo's friend Jason and what he might have found out.

"I went to high school with his brother, the one you helped get treatment for," Jeff said to Lorenzo. "He was always a pretty wild kid, getting in trouble, getting a girl pregnant, that kind of thing. He almost never came to class and when he showed up, he was always clowning around. I only knew him slightly."

"From what I hear about him now, he's straightened up and is running the family sheep operation," said Lorenzo.

"Good for him," said Jeff. "I wouldn't have guessed that was possible. He seemed hopeless."

"I guess you can take credit for that turnaround, Lorenzo," I said. "You got him into a treatment program and I guess it took."

"Maybe so. We'll ask Jason when we see him tonight."

"Where are you guys meeting him?" asked Jeff.

"Some old barn on their ranch," said Lorenzo. He took a piece of paper from his shirt pocket and handed it to Jeff.

"Yeah, I know that barn. It's really remote. I think the main Arriaga operation is several miles away. I guess that's why he picked the spot. One thing, though: that land borders on Dickson White's land. You'll need to be careful you don't cross over the boundary. You found out the other day how touchy he is about his territory—he's got just enough of the old cattle baron mentality in him to think it would be fine to shoot both of you and claim you were trespassers."

"And he'd probably get away with it, if the sheriff had anything to say about it," I said, shaking my head.

"You boys want some dessert?" Dot had returned. She barely acknowledged Jeff and me but was looking at Lorenzo.

"How can I resist you," he said. "I mean, as a saleswoman. Do you have any fruit pies?"

"You better believe it, honey. I'll cut you the biggest piece of Dutch apple pie you've ever eaten. When you're eatin' it, you'll think you've died and gone to heaven."

"Sold," said Lorenzo.

She turned to leave.

"Oh, miss?" I said.

She turned around with an annoyed look on her face.

"Jeff will have the same, but I just want coffee."

"Oh, sure, hon. Comin' right up." She walked away, whistling to herself.

CHAPTER 25

THAT NIGHT JUST AFTER TEN, Lorenzo and I drove along an unpaved farm road to the meeting with Jason Arriaga. Luckily for me and my car, Lorenzo had rented a four-wheel drive Jeep which could take the countless ruts and potholes better than my rental car. Jeff had assured us that the road formed the border between Arriaga land and Dickson White's spread. I hoped so. We rode in silence for ten minutes because the noise from the car hitting bottom and the whine of the four-wheel drive straining to lift us out of deep and muddy gullies made it hard to be heard.

Lorenzo kept turning on the headlights to make sure he was following the road. When we reached a fork in the road, Lorenzo stopped the car and switched on a flashlight to look at the map Jeff had made for us.

"Let's see if we can tell where we are," he said. "Too bad there's no moon tonight. It's as dark as a dungeon."

"One advantage of the darkness is that it does make it hard to see us, in case White or one of his men is out riding the range tonight."

"There is that, I guess."

Lorenzo followed Jeff's penciled line with his finger to the fork where we had stopped. "I hope your buddy is as good a journalist as he is a mapmaker," said Lorenzo. "This map is really good."

"I train my people to cope with all eventualities in life," I said, smiling.

"Okay, it seems we go to the right and in another five minutes or so, the old barn should be in front of us."

Lorenzo gunned the engine and the car lurched up out of a particularly deep rut. The wheels spun for a few seconds and then moved the car forward.

"I may sue for whiplash," I yelled at Lorenzo, who just gritted his teeth and kept driving.

In about five minutes, I could see the barn sitting right next to the road. It was two stories tall with a wide door in front and a large opening just above it, I assumed for moving hay into trucks parked below. The wooden boards on the walls were so old they had turned gray from years of hard winter weather—low temperatures and a lot of snow. Wind had played its part too: the whole building sagged to the left.

Lorenzo pulled around to the side and drove as far as the tall weeds would allow. We both got out.

"This building is great," he said. "I mean, it's old but it has real character, like fine wine. . . ."

"Or aging professors," I added.

"You're not old, Tom," he said, smiling. "You're just . . ."

"Careful, now, counselor. Our future friendship depends on your choice of words."

"Extremely experienced? Dilapidated? Stately? Archaic? All knowing?"

"Just stick to old."

After finding the large front doors locked, we stepped through an opening in a side wall between splintered boards. Walking to the center of the barn, we both ducked as a bat or a bird skittered near our heads.

"Jesus, Mary and Joseph, as we Catholics say!" muttered Lorenzo.

"Like. What. Ever. As the university Valley Girls in my class say."

We sat down on a wooden bench at the far end of the building.

"What time's your friend supposed to be here?"

"He said 10:30, but Jesus has always been late."

"How can you say that about your dearest friend and first love," quipped a voice from above.

We looked up just as a figure shimmied down a rope from a platform above where we were sitting.

"Ta da."

Jesus or Jason Arriaga was taller than Lorenzo and a bit heavier. He did match him in looks—dark hair and eyes, fine features—although the extra flesh detracted from his overall handsomeness. He rushed over to Lorenzo and grabbed him around the neck and kissed him hard on the lips.

Lorenzo staggered back. "Whoa, Jason. Let me get my breath." He reached over and shook his friend's hand. "And this is my good friend, Tom."

Arriaga had not acknowledged me till then and still barely glanced in my direction. "Oh, hi. Kind of old for you, Renzo." He winked at me. "But lots of experience in those years, I'll bet."

"Look, Jason . . ." Lorenzo interjected.

"I'm Jesus for this trip, honey. Anglicizing my name really freaks my brother out. I play along with him for the sake of my mother, who still thinks I'll get married and bring her lots of little *nietos* to sit at her knee and hear stories about Basque history or other shit like that."

"Okay, got it," replied Lorenzo. "So, your brother is still living a clean life—no drugs, no booze?"

"You put him on the right path. He's still a jerk, but now he's a jerk without a drug or alcohol problem. And he's doing a good job of running the ranch. When I see a sheep now, I think only of eating lamb chops." He walked over to Lorenzo and put his arm around his waist. "Speaking of somewhat carnal subjects, why don't you and I climb up into the loft for a little roll in the hay?"

Even in the dim light, I could see Lorenzo blush in embarrassment at his friend's behavior. "Look, Jesus. I told you that was over. In fact, we were never together, except in your mind. Get over it. We've got more important things to do."

Jesus Arriaga sighed and turned away. "Okay, okay. I'll quit making you uncomfortable, as much as I love to do it. You know you make it very easy with your steely resolve to trudge on through life without me." He touched his hand to his forehead as if playing a role on stage as a femme fatale and quoted: "I have always been blessed with the kindness of strangers, but not these two strangers."

"Blanche Du Bois you are not, Jesus," said Lorenzo. "Now, quit clowning around and tell us what you found out."

"Not until you agree to have dinner with me in Portland or Bend or some other civilized place where I can gaze into your eyes and hold your hand. That's certainly not possible in this bastion of rednecks."

"Dinner in Portland before you go back to San Francisco," said Lorenzo with a sigh to emphasize his reluctance. "A place of your choice and my treat."

"Goodie. You've made this queen very happy." Arriaga cleared his throat and lowered his voice. "Okay, men. Let me give you my report in my ranch hand voice. I learned to talk this way to keep the cowboys from chasing me around the campfire. That is, when they weren't balling the sheep. You know, there's a lot of *Brokeback Mountain* time out here on the range. But I digress." He winked at me again. "Okay, pardners, here's the scoop. My brother thinks that Dickson White is stealing both cattle and sheep from us and other ranchers and herding them onto a remote part of his ranch for rebranding before he sells them and ships them out on the sly. I hear he tracks them from a helicopter and has some kind of new laser branding tool that removes the old brand and puts his in its place. The whole process is done quickly and at night. The big rigs are waiting and the animals are out of here in minutes."

"I don't get it," I said. "He's wealthy already. Why does he need more?"

"Honey, people like that are greedy with a capital G," said Arriaga. "The more he gets, the more he wants. Plus, he's buying more and more land up here, gobbling up small ranches right and left. He wants to be the 'go to' guy in the county. My brother says he's already got the sheriff in his pocket, which helps to get his son out of trouble when necessary. Got a girl pregnant and left her in the lurch a few years ago."

"That's Penny Brando, a waitress in the café where we ate, Lorenzo," I said. "She seems like a sweet kid, and my friend Jeff

Walls says she's struggling to raise her kid without help from the White family."

"Junior White's a real nasty character," continued Arriaga. "Been in trouble all his life. I remember him in school—handsome as the devil, but no good. He usually led the pack of kids who taunted me for being, let us say, different. And I was older and bigger. Sissy that I was, though, I'd never fight back. My brother would always step in and rescue me. He hated me for putting him in that kind of situation. That's why I got out of here as soon as I could and have never looked back." Arriaga looked sad as he remembered those bad times. He shook his head. "It's not easy being gay, dear Renzo. Am I right?"

Lorenzo nodded his head but said nothing.

I broke the silence. "So, White's an old-fashioned rustler using high-tech equipment."

"Seems so," said Arriaga.

"Does any of this take place on Steens Mountain? I mean, that's where my friend's husband went missing. My theory is that he was hiking up there and saw something somebody did not like him to see."

"And that somebody could very well be Dickson White or someone who works for Dickson White," added Lorenzo.

"Even though White's cattle are near here, it doesn't make sense that Mike Tateman would be hiking over here and see something he shouldn't have," I said. "I found a coin I think was his, up on the mountain. That makes me think he was up there just before he disappeared."

"Yeah," said Arriaga. "That doesn't make any sense at all. All I know is what my brother told me. I'll keep looking around the ranch and asking questions in my innocent, somewhat mincing, way."

"Thanks, Jesus. We both appreciate this very much."

"I presume I will get my reward when we get back to civilization?" He laughed and winked at me, then looked at his watch. "I'd better get back so I can tuck my mama into bed."

"So, what do we have here?" said a voice from the opening in the wall where Lorenzo and I had come into the barn. "Three fuckin' queers who are just askin' to have me ream their asses."

CHAPTER 26

THREE MEN WALKED INTO THE BARN: the deputy, Clay Murchison;
the cowboy who had been with him at the Frenchglen Hotel,
Marty something; and a third guy who I assumed was Junior
White.

Surprisingly, Jesus Arriaga walked right up to White to con-
front him.

"You know, Junior—if I may be so bold as to address you with
your nickname—this barn happens to be on my family's land.
Although I don't intend to press it, you three are trespassing. It
might be best if you . . ."

"Shut your fuckin' trap, you prevert!" White's words were
slurred.

"The word is *pervert,* you moron. But I guess you never did
take the time to get an education. You were too busy getting innocent girls in trouble, then leaving them to fend for themselves."

Hearing that, White lunged at Jesus, who stepped aside so
that the man fell flat on his face. Both Marty and Clay rushed to
help him to his feet.

"I told you we shouldn't have come up here tonight," said Marty.

"Shut up, Marty," hissed Clay. "You're in this as much as we are."

Jesus had walked over to Lorenzo and me, and the three of us stood facing the other three. All of them were clearly drunk and probably not much of a threat to us. But it worried me that Clay Murchison was in uniform and wearing his gun.

White struggled to his feet, pushing away the helping hands of his buddies. "Leave me alone! I can lick these fairies with one hand tied behind me!"

"Look, White," said Lorenzo. "If you just turn around and walk out of here, we'll forget this happened. We won't mention it to your father and, Deputy Clay, we won't say anything to your uncle." He turned to face Clay, who looked surprised that Lorenzo knew who he was.

"You know, I could haul you all in for trespassing on private property," said Jesus.

"And the private property happens to be mine and my brother's." Another voice came from behind us, and a taller and thinner version of Jesus Arriaga stepped into the barn from a gaping hole in the opposite side. He was followed by ten men who looked, by the way they were dressed, to be sheep herders. All were carrying rifles.

"Antonio Arriaga," he said, as he shook my hand. He was completely ignoring the three louts in front of us. He moved toward Lorenzo. "Good to see you again, *amigo*." They embraced. Then he nodded his head, and the men with him fanned out along the perimeter of the barn.

Junior White was looking nervous. "You can't just come in here and do this. My dad'll clean your clock. . . . Clay here will arrest you for tres . . ."

"As I told you before, my stupid friend, you can't arrest a man for walking around his own property. You three are the trespassers."

"He may be right, Junior," said Marty. "I never worked any of your dad's cows over this far. Let's just leave now, like he says."

"Shut up, Marty. We'll leave when I say we leave."

Antonio nodded his head again, and the men around the perimeter raised their rifles.

"Okay, okay. I give up," said the deputy, raising his hands in the air. "Come on Junior, let's just get on out of here."

The younger White bent over as if to brush the dust off his clothes. As he hunched over, he made a run at Arriaga, his head down like a battering ram. Antonio turned to face him, a look of pity on his face. As White passed in front of me, I put out my foot and tripped him. Once again, he fell face down in the dirt. This time, he landed more forcefully than before so that his open mouth was now filled with dirt. He started coughing and spitting. His friends rushed over and pulled him to his feet. They had to drag him out through the side opening.

"This ain't over, Arriaga. I'll git you for this," White shouted over his shoulder.

"The correct words are *isn't* and *get*. Not only are you a bully but you are an ungrammatical one at that," sneered Jesus.

Antonio walked over to his brother and slapped him across the face. "Why do you continue to bring dishonor on our family? Your mere presence is an insult to the memory of our illustrious ancestors and our father who worked his ass off for us!"

Jesus rubbed his face. "Don't give me that 'blessed are the ancestors' shit," he shouted, his eyes flashing in anger. "I appreciate their sacrifices as much as you do. I'd come back here and work the sheep or till the soil if you'd let me. You're ashamed of me, so I stay away. Do you think I wanted things to turn out this way? Don't you think I wish I was more like you?" He turned to Lorenzo and me as if to draw us onto his side of the argument. "However, I can't see myself in peasant garb—drawstring pants and a white shirt made out of flour sack, a straw hat on my head. I'd need something from Abercrombie's. Now THAT might have possibilities!"

That broke the tension, and all four of us started laughing. Then we moved outside to continue our discussion.

"I'll keep trying to find out as much as I can about White Senior's operation," said Antonio. "It doesn't make sense that your friend saw some cattle rustling over here when Jesus tells me you have reason to think he was up on the Steens when he disappeared."

"Yeah, I agree," I said. "I found this up on the mountain." I handed him the Indian head penny. "I'm thinking it was his lucky piece. If so, it proves he was up there, but what he saw I don't know."

"I guess you got nowhere with the sheriff."

"He didn't even go through the motions to look for Mike Tateman."

"You know, you might try the chief deputy, Hank French. He's as honest as Sheriff Murchison is crooked. If you lay out the case for him, I bet he'll help you. That is, if he thinks you're onto something. He would like to run for sheriff someday, but for the past many years, no one has had a chance against Murchison because Dickson White backed him."

"Thanks for helping us, Tonio," said Lorenzo. "I owe you."

"Look, counselor, you saved me from my evil half a while back, and I owe you big time. If it wasn't for you getting me into that treatment program, I'd be dead or a bum on Skid Row somewhere. But I don't get why you're involved here. My crazy brother always has stars in his eyes when he talks about you, so I never get a straight story from him."

"You got *that* right, bro," said Jesus. "I'm not capable of telling a *straight* story, only *bent* ones."

"Tom is an old friend and my sometime client," said Lorenzo. "His friend hired me to help him find out what happened to her husband."

"Ah, I see," said Antonio. He nodded to his men, and they walked toward several pickups parked in a clearing away from the barn. "I'll be in touch, my friends," he said, as he walked away. "I'll see you at home, Jesus. You need to be there to give mama her cup of tea. For God knows what reason, she still likes you."

"So, where do we go from here?" asked Jesus, after his brother was gone.

"*We* does not include you, Jesus," said Lorenzo. "You have done enough for us already, and we thank you for that. But after this incident here tonight, I think you need to keep a low profile until you leave."

"But I'd like to keep seeing you, Renzo." Jesus was pouting, his lips quivering.

"We'll have dinner in Portland before you leave the state. Call me and I'll set it up. How long are you staying?"

"Just another few days. I can only take this blissful rural life for so long. I need the danger and depravity of the big city—sex and the single guy, and all that." He grabbed Lorenzo again for one last embrace. "You sure know how to break a guy's heart. Good-bye." He glanced at me. "Nice to meet you too, Don, was it?"

CHAPTER 27

THE TRILL OF MY CELL PHONE woke me up the next morning. In the bed on the opposite side of the room, Lorenzo was snoring softly. We had arrived at Jeff's house so late, he had insisted that Lorenzo stay over.

"Hello."

"Tom, it's Margot."

I cleared my throat.

"Did I wake you?"

"No, I was just getting up. How are you?"

"Oh, I'm okay. Some days are better than others. This day isn't too bad, so far. I wanted to talk to you about a couple of things. I'm sorry it's taken me so long to call you. Life has been hell lately."

I stood up and walked down the stairs to the living room.

"Are you there, Tom?"

"Yeah, sorry, I was just moving to a better place to talk. What's up?"

"First of all, in your message you asked if Mike had a lucky piece, an Indian head penny."

"Yes. Did he?"

"Yes, he was never without it. That and a cap from Northwestern University Law School. He got his law degree there and wore the hat a lot. His grandfather gave him the penny for good luck. I gather you found it?"

"Not the cap, but the penny, yes, on top of Steens Mountain."

"So that proves he was up there. I'm so glad. It means the world to me that you've found something. That stupid sheriff has been running around in circles and not turning up anything. He called me yesterday."

"He did? That's a surprise."

"That's the other thing I wanted to tell you. He was very nice and said that he was doing everything he could to find Mike."

"You don't believe that, of course."

"No, of course not. But I played along and thanked him for his efforts. I bit my tongue several times to keep from telling him what I really thought of him and his non-search."

"Did he mention about meeting me or that he knew I was over here looking for Mike?"

"No, he said nothing about you. That surprised me because I know you've seen him several times. I thought it best not to mention you."

"Yeah, he doesn't like me very much. I guess he was just covering his ass by calling you. Maybe he thinks that one call will smooth things over."

"No chance of that happening. What else can you tell me, Tom?"

"Lorenzo is here, and the two of us are making progress sorting this out. We have reason to believe that a local big shot may be involved. Dickson White. You ever hear of him?"

"No, I don't think so."

"He's a rancher who has good political connections and the sheriff in his pocket. He's got a nasty son who gets into trouble all the time. And then there's the sheriff's nephew."

"Whew. Sounds complicated."

"It is. And I'm still sorting this all out. I'll let you know when I have anything solid to report. Or when I find Mike's . . ." I stopped myself.

"It's okay, Tom. I know he's dead. I felt that strongly after the first few days, but I guess you never lose hope in situations like this." Margot's voice was getting quivery.

"Yeah, I'm afraid so. I'm sorry, Margot."

"I'm going to hang up now, Tom. I'm not feeling all that well. Thanks to you and to Lorenzo."

The line went dead.

"I take it that was your friend?" Lorenzo had come downstairs, a sheet wrapped around him.

I nodded. "Poor gal. Her loss is the kind you never get over."

"Don't I know it," he said, shaking his head.

I made coffee, and we sat down at Jeff's kitchen table to drink it.

"I think we've made progress, Tom, don't you?" Lorenzo said.

"Yes, but there's a lot more to do."

"I really need to get back to Salem and tend to my practice. Most of my clients are desperate on their best days and need my help to stay in this country or deal with an unscrupulous landlord or boss."

"I know you've got to go. You've really been a great help. I couldn't have gotten the information from the Arriagas without you. But I can take it from here. I'm going to try to make contact with the good deputy. Hank French, I think his name is. If I need help from a legal standpoint later, I'll call you."

A knock on the door interrupted our conversation. I walked over and opened it.

"What's an African American cowgirl have to do to get a cup of coffee around here," asked Trina Hutchins.

"God, Trina, I thought we were working undercover over here," said Lorenzo, smiling.

"Honey, there's no reason to hide it if you've got it," she answered, waving a hand in the direction of her ample cleavage. "I figure these crackers won't arrest me if they're staring at my boobs." It was impossible for Trina to dress in an inconspicuous way, even if she tried, which I doubted she ever did. She had on jeans that were so tight it looked as if she had been poured into them. Her sequined top gleamed in the sunlight that was coming through the window by the table where she sat drinking coffee and eating the toast I made for her. Mercifully, she wasn't wearing her cowboy hat.

"So, what did you find out?" I asked.

"Well," she leaned in close to the two of us, "I do know more about birds than I ever cared to. Birds are all that overweight couple and their skinny friend think of—morning, noon, and night. They did provide me good cover, though. I pretended to be interested in what they had to say and took a lot of notes."

"Good girl," said Lorenzo. "But did you find out anything useful to our investigation?"

"First, let me say that this is one beautiful place. It makes a city girl like me appreciate the outdoors a lot more than I ever did before. Anyway, I couldn't do much looking around up on top of the mountain. I wanted to break away from the birders and really hunt for signs of your friend's husband. But that Herb guy, he was always trailing after me, spelling the names of birds we were seeing and watching me write them down in my little black book." She pulled the book out of her purse and held it in the air.

"And catching a sneak peak at your cleavage," said Lorenzo, laughing and shaking his head.

"No doubt," I said. "I'm sure Herb loves Sue, but you and your," I cleared my throat, "*attributes* are just too tempting."

"Herb's really harmless. He and Sue offered to give me a ride into town. I remembered that you said your former student runs the newspaper, so we stopped there for directions. I did find out some useful information at the hotel, however," she continued. "Last night before dinner, I was chatting up Mr. Bates, the manager, while he was working in the kitchen. I danced around the subject of Mike Tateman and kind of led him into talking about what people do when they hike up the mountain—like I was interested in exploring up there. Before long, he was telling me what people had told him. He doesn't seem to have done much hiking himself. Too busy with the hotel, I guess. Anyway, after a while, he mentioned that a guy showed up soon after the hotel opened for the season, a month or so ago. He said it was really too early to go up the mountain with all the snow that was still on the road, especially near the top."

"That sounds like it could have been Mike Tateman. That's about when he came here."

"So, is there more to the story?" asked Lorenzo, some impatience in his voice.

"Oh yeah, there is," she said. "Sorry, I do tend to get carried away. I like to embellish . . ."

"Trina. Get on with your story!"

"Mr. Bates said that this man—probably Mike Tateman—wanted to know all about some canyon where wild horses run. We saw some horses while we were up there, but they weren't in any canyon. They were running around in the open. On kind of rangey-looking ground."

"Spoken like a true cowgirl," Lorenzo said, laughing.

"Those horses he was talking about would be the Kiger mustangs I've read about," I said. "They are descended from the horses the Spanish conquistadors brought with them to North America in the 17th century. The BLM keeps them separate from the horses you saw to protect the purity of the breed. People are discouraged from going into that canyon."

"That's got to be where Mike Tateman is," said Trina.

"Or his body," added Lorenzo. "Not much chance he's alive after all this time."

"I just told Margot that on the phone, and she agreed with me. If I can find any signs of him in there, I'll get someone to conduct a search and then a recovery operation."

"You can't go there alone, Tom," he said. "But I've got to get back to Salem."

"I could go with . . ." Trina started to say, but Lorenzo cut her off.

"No, you can't. You're beautiful and sweet and smart and a lot of other great things, but an undercover operative in southeastern Oregon you are not. Besides, I've got some more important work for you to do for me."

Trina frowned as if she did not agree with her boss but then nodded her head slowly. "Yeah, I know you're right, but I wanted so much to help Tom's friend." Her eyes were misting over.

I reached over and squeezed Trina's hand. "You've been a great help by finding out that Mike Tateman was asking Bates at the hotel about the canyon where the wild horses were. Lorenzo and I were at a dead end."

Trina stood up and squared her shoulders. "Okay, boss. What've you got for me next?"

"Many of my clients are farm workers and they've told me repeatedly about the terrible condition of the houses they have to live in. I want you to check out the situation, make witness statements, and take plenty of photos. How does that sound?"

"I do speak enough Spanish to get by, and I could wear some not-so-stylish jeans, a blue work shirt, and a scarf on my head."

"No jewelry. No makeup."

"I think I could pass for Cuban."

The three of us smiled at the thought.

CHAPTER 28

LORENZO AND TRINA LEFT SOON AFTER I agreed that I would check in with him every night by seven to report my findings and assure him that I was all right.

My plan was to approach the apparently only honest lawman in the area, Chief Deputy Hank French. But first I wanted to go into Kiger Gorge to look around.

Even I was not foolish enough to go up there alone. I asked Jeff Walls to go with me when I met him at the Cattlemen's Café later.

"I'd love to do it," he said, "but this is my deadline day. I just can't get away. I've always planned to go back into that canyon and have kept putting it off, but it can't be today."

"So, you've been there?"

"Yeah, when I was a teenager. My dad took me there as a kind of rite of passage."

"Did you walk over hot lava or something?" I laughed.

"Not that bad. He thought I should stay there overnight by myself."

"Spooky."

"Yeah, definitely."

"What happened? Did you do it?"

"No, klutz that I am, I twisted my ankle. We had to come back out pretty fast. We never got to do it again. I got busy with school and work . . . and then my dad was dead." Jeff shook his head.

"What's all this sadness?" Penny Brando handed us each a menu and a glass of iced tea. "I believe you had lemon in yours, professor." She was smiling and much more relaxed than when I first met her.

"Pen, do you remember when I went into Kiger Gorge when we were still kids and was going to spend the night?"

"Yeah, kind of, I guess."

"I was telling Professor Martindale about twisting my ankle so I didn't get to go."

"Why you talkin' about that stuff now?" she asked, a look of fear in her eyes. "You aren't going to go in there again, are you?"

"You ever been in that canyon, Penny?" I asked.

"Once on a dare, I went with a boy."

Jeff looked up from the menu. "Don't tell me, let me guess. Junior White lured you up there. Is that where you lost your virginity?"

Penny blanched and ran to the back of the café.

"Jeff," I said. "Was that necessary?"

"That bum ruined her life. She was a nice girl before he got hold of her. He flashed all his money and, apparently, his dick, and she was lost forever. Now she's got a sick kid and no money to care for him, and she's working in a dead-end job with no future."

Everyone in the café was staring at us. The older waitress, Dot, hurried over. "What did you say to our fair Penny, young man?" she demanded.

"I just told the truth," he said. He looked at me. "All of a sudden, I've lost my appetite."

"Look, hon," said Dot, "let me fix you boys some nice tuna sandwiches and I'll throw in some pie. How does that sound?"

Jeff looked up at her with misty eyes and blew his nose. "Yeah, I guess."

"That will be perfect," I said, smiling at her kindness.

Just then, a tall man in a sheriff's uniform walked in the front door. He sat down at a table by the window and nodded in our direction.

"Is that Hank French?" I asked Jeff.

"That's the man. Only decent lawman we've got around here, that's for sure."

"Can you introduce me on our way out?"

"I will do that."

Dot arrived with our sandwiches, and we ate them and the pie quickly.

I put a twenty dollar bill on the table, winking at Dot as we walked past her. "I'll take care of our boy."

"You see that you do. He's someone special."

Jeff blushed but said nothing.

"Make this seem casual, I mean meeting Sheriff French," I whispered.

We walked toward the door and then Jeff stopped at the front table and acted surprised. "Oh, hi, Sheriff French. How ya doing? I want you to meet my old professor from the university, Tom Martindale."

French got up and shook my hand with one of those bone crushing grips you don't forget. He was tall and slender and looked good in his expertly tailored uniform. As I recalled from my encounters with his boss, Sheriff Murchison, *his* ample belly had protruded over his barely visible belt.

"Sit down," he said. "I usually eat alone, but I've always enjoyed Jeff's company. Good to meet you, Mr. Martindale. Or is it Professor Martindale?"

"Tom is fine, sheriff."

"Then I'm Hank, short for Henry."

Dot placed a huge breakfast in front of the sheriff: pancakes, bacon, sausage, eggs, and potatoes.

"How do you keep so trim?" I asked, gesturing at this plate.

"Oh, easy. I run a lot, and I also get my exercise chasing bad guys."

We all laughed and the sheriff dug into his food.

I leaned close to French. "I've wanted to meet you. I've got something I need to talk to you about, and it's kind of confidential."

French stopped chewing and looked at me with a frown on his face. "Is this a law enforcement matter?"

"Yes, I guess it is."

"I really don't like to do business when I'm eating."

He seemed to stiffen a bit, but Jeff broke in to ease the tension. "Tom needs your help. He's tried the sheriff and hasn't gotten any help. I'm sure that doesn't surprise you. You and I are friends, Hank, so I know you trust me. Hell, after all the years we've known each other, I hope you trust me."

French resumed eating and seemed to relax. "Okay, okay. You don't need to remind me that I trust you, Jeff. I guess this'll just have to be one of those 'any friend of yours is a friend of mine' kind of thing." He looked at me.

I started to tell him about Mike Tateman and the sheriff's handling of the case, but he held up his hand. "Not here. How long you going to be around?"

"Another few days—or longer—depending on the outcome of our conversation."

"Sounds serious." He thought for a moment. "Tell you what. I've got to go to Bend later today for some God-awful retirement dinner for the police chief there. Then I've got some training sessions to do for my men tomorrow morning. How about I meet the two of you tomorrow night at your place, Jeff? I'll come in that back road down by the creek so no one will see me." He glanced around. "In this town, even the walls have ears. People on the force might wonder why I'm going to your place at night if they see me turn onto your road."

"You mean people like Sheriff Murchison and his idiot nephew, Clay," said Jeff.

"You said it, Jeff, I didn't." Then he smiled and finished his breakfast. When we walked out the door, he was ordering a piece of apple pie from Dot.

CHAPTER 29

AFTER JEFF HAD GONE TO WORK and I had eaten breakfast, I drove back to Frenchglen to say my goodbyes to Herb and Sue and their friend, Catherine Rickbone. Trina had said they were still there. I also wanted to check out Kiger Gorge. I pulled into the parking area just as the three of them were walking down the steps.

"Well, by golly, you are a sight for sore eyes," said Herb.

I walked over to the three of them. Herb shook my hand vigorously and the two women hugged me, even the sedate Ms. Rickbone.

"We thought you'd gone," said Sue. "I have to say I was a bit disappointed that you didn't say goodbye. Those other nice people—that Mr. Madrid and his wife, Trina—left in kind of a hurry."

"She went with us up the mountain, by golly," said Herb. "Did a good job keeping up for a city girl. A nice little gal and quite a looker in that cowgirl outfit."

"I don't think she'll ever be a birder, though," said Ms. Rickbone, shaking her head.

"I'll bet she just wanted to be outdoors for a while," I said. "We city people crave the outdoors once in a while. In fact, that's why I came back. I wanted to go up the Steens again. I am really glad you three are here; I was going up alone one last time before I left, but now I'll have your great company."

Occasionally, I shave the truth a bit to get what I want. In truth, they would be excellent cover for me to go back up the mountain without arousing any suspicion, should the sheriff or his nephew drop by.

"Oh, there's Mr. Bates," said Sue, with a wave as the manager of the hotel walked down the steps toward us.

"I didn't expect to see you again, Mr. Martindale," he said, shaking my hand. "Did you know those other people, Mr. and Mrs. Madrid?"

Time for another lie. "Not before I met them here."

"Oh, too bad. She left this small notebook in their room, and I thought you could take it to them."

How could Trina be so careless? What was in the notebook? Had Bates read it?

"You know what?" I said. "He gave me his card because he might be willing to take one of my students as an intern." I waved a business card, my own. "I may be seeing him next week in Salem. I'll take it to him."

Before Bates could object, I grabbed the notebook out of his hand and put it into my pocket.

"Oh, well, all right. That'll solve my problem since they didn't leave a forwarding address." He seemed to dismiss the issue of the notebook and turned to the others. "You goin' back up the mountain again?"

"Yes, by golly," said Herb. "One last time, and Tom here is going with us."

"You checking back in then, Mr. Martindale? I've got one room left for tonight."

"No, unfortunately, I promised to stay with one of my former students in Burns tonight, and then I've got to get back to the valley. But thanks for offering. I really enjoyed the times I stayed here."

"Well, by golly," said Herb, "we best be getting on our way before it gets real hot."

"It will be cooler up on top, and you might even see some leftover snow," said Bates, as he turned and walked back into the hotel. "See you all for dinner."

We walked to Herb's car and got in. I offered to sit in the back seat but Sue insisted that I ride up front with Herb. He backed out and peeled rubber as he sped down the road.

"Herb, what's gotten into you?" shouted Sue from the rear.

* * * * *

The view from the top of Steens Mountain was as breathtaking that day as ever. I walked up to the edge as I had on my previous visits and enjoyed the whole panoply of magnificent vistas that were in view. As before, the colors of the distant mountains contrasted with the desert below in an ethereal way that was hard to describe. High above, the billowy white clouds cast random shadows on the ground.

Being a city person all my life, I had never really felt the need to commune with nature to the extent of camping out in remote places or hiking great distances to get there. But I've always liked the writings of Henry David Thoreau, and I have to admit that I feel a kinship with him and his life in the woods every time I visit

Walden Pond. Improbable as it sounds, I think a lot of writers dream of a simple room in which to work—a plain wooden desk, clean sheets of paper, an inkwell and dip pen at the ready. Well, maybe not the inkwell and dip pen.

While I wasn't planning to pitch a tent up here on the mountain, just standing here did inspire me.

"Not a lot of birds up here," said Herb, as he walked up next to me. "I think we'd like to go farther down."

"Fine by me," I said. "Can you let me off at Kiger Gorge? I think it's over that way." I pointed in the direction of where I thought the gorge was located. "I'd like to look around there a bit. Maybe you could pick me up in a couple of hours."

The four of us got back in the car and Herb peeled rubber once again.

"Herb," yelled Sue from the rear. "What's gotten into you!"

He smiled and gunned the engine even more. We were at the sign for Kiger Gorge in a few minutes. He stopped and I got out of the car, the dust from the road swirling around me.

"You gonna hike down in there, Tom?" asked Herb, while leaning across the seat. "Why're you interested in that area?"

"Just curious about that herd of wild horses you told me about that the government keeps separate from the ones we saw farther down. Looks like an easy hike down. See you in a couple of hours. That'll be noon. I've got a couple of water bottles and a hat. Don't worry about me—I'll be fine."

As the car drove away, I thought of Mike Tateman. He probably set off in just this way—fully prepared for a nice hike into an interesting-looking canyon with no thought of the harm to come. I was less sanguine, but I had to find out if this was where he died.

The way down into the canyon was a gradual slope, which made my walk easy. After several minutes, it flattened out. This was no Grand Canyon, with its steep sides and forbidding depth. Instead, the gorge was a wide-open space and the walls slanted out from the bottom, which made the sides seem shorter than they actually were.

The barren terrain gradually turned into green foliage, which was muddy in spots due to the few remaining patches of snow. I heard running water ahead and soon came to a stream. I stepped across it easily and walked on to where the canyon was wider. With water from the stream, this large area was lush and green.

As I gazed up the walls of the canyon, a movement to my left caught my eye. A huge stallion lifted his head and looked at me. He was larger than any of the wild horses I had seen a month before on Dickson White's ranch. He was dun colored with zebra-like stripes on his upper legs and shoulders and a stripe running down the middle of his back. His mane and tail were long and black and silver colored. He was magnificent, and I remembered reading about *Mesteno*, the stallion that the other horses could be traced back to and whose name means "stray" or "feral" in Spanish.

I stared at him for several minutes, transfixed by his beauty. After a while, I heard a rustling coming from behind him and then five mares broke through the bushes to surround him and, presumably, to admire him. His harem had come to show off for their master.

A smaller version of him, a foal that barely came up to the lower part of his body, came scampering up to him and began to nip at his tail. The stallion tolerated this annoyance for a few seconds, then butted the foal away. One of the mares nudged the youngster back a bit away from his father.

Just then, I sneezed. All of the horses froze in place and looked in my direction. If the stallion had tolerated my presence before, he now decided I was an enemy to be gotten rid of. He began to walk toward me, at first slowly. I backed away for a few seconds, then turned and broke into a run. Although I doubted I could outrun a horse, I knew I had to try. I ran as fast as I could toward a small opening in the canyon wall I had noticed earlier.

The horse probably only wanted to get me away from his mares and the foal and would not actually try to trample me, but my hunches don't always turn out the way I think. I could see the headline now: **FLAKY PROFESSOR KILLED BY HORSE IN REMOTE CANYON. LATEST INCIDENT IN A CAREER FILLED WITH QUESTIONABLE CONDUCT**. My tenure would certainly be revoked posthumously.

The horse ran ahead of me, then doubled back and crossed my path. He seemed to be playing with me and enjoying every minute of it. I would head in one direction and he would cut me off. The same would happen when I tried another route.

After a few minutes, he had maneuvered me to a spot along the wall, just below the opening I had been trying to reach. I turned to face him.

He reared up as if to accentuate his superiority. On his hind legs, he looked forty feet tall. I envisioned one of those hooves coming down on me and splitting my skull. I braced for the blow.

At that moment, I heard a faint rattling sound. I turned my head in time to see a large rattlesnake poised to strike the stallion on one leg. The horse leapt to one side, and the snake missed his mark.

All that commotion gave me enough time to clamber up the rock to the ledge I had been heading for. As the horse moved away from me and the snake, I turned and stepped into the opening of a cave. I walked in and turned to look at the horse. He turned and gazed at me for a few seconds, then trotted back to where his mares had resumed their grazing. He had accomplished his duties as the king of the herd and gotten rid of this two-legged bad guy—me.

I decided to wait a while before I chanced a departure. I figured the horses would move along eventually. I walked deeper into the cave and turned on my flashlight. The rock walls were covered with moss and some graffiti. "A stud in the Steens. Johnny loves Gloria." "Won't you be my stallion forever. JR loves CA." Stuff like that.

I sat down on a rock to drink some water. I shined the light up to the top of the cave and then around the walls. The light caught something shiny at the far end of the cave. I got up and walked over to it.

What I found was a dark object—a man's leather wallet with a large reddish splotch on the side. I realized that the light had bounced off the edge of a plastic sleeve inside the wallet. When I opened the wallet, I saw that it held an Oregon driver's license issued to one Michael Tateman of Portland.

CHAPTER 30

EVEN WITH ALL THE COMMOTION with the stallion, I still got back to the meeting point with Herb within the two-hour time frame we had set. I got out of the canyon without incident and did not see the horses. Herb did not ask me what I had been doing in the gorge and I didn't tell him. We drove back to Frenchglen and I said my goodbyes to him, Sue, and Catherine Rickbone.

After I returned to Jeff's house in Burns, I told him what I had found. We agreed that I needed to talk to Hank French, the chief deputy, as soon as possible. He had earlier agreed to meet us tonight, but we both felt we had to talk to him sooner than that. Jeff said he would call Hank at the office as if checking on a routine police matter and figure out how the deputy and I could meet.

"I'll call him on his cell," said Jeff, as we sat down in his office. "No one will be monitoring that." He kept his voice low so his aunt who was sitting outside at the reception desk would not hear him. It also helped that she was on the phone, taking down details for a classified ad in her usual loud voice.

"I know that sounds expensive, Mabel, but you're just gonna have to pay it if you want to sell that old dining table and chairs. Only five chairs? Hmmm. Tables usually have an even number of chairs. Yes, you'll have a lot of people traipsing through your house. Look, do you want to sell this stuff or not? Okay, then. Get Willie to move it all to the back porch. Okay, then. I'll send you a bill, or you can stop by next time you're in town."

She started muttering something after hanging up but was interrupted by the front door opening. She pushed her chair back and, presumably, walked to the counter. "Yes, sir. What can I do you for?"

Jeff motioned for me to close the door to his office. "Sheriff French? This is Jeff Walls. I've got something to tell you that is kind of urgent. Can you meet us for lunch at the Cattlemen's today? How about one, after the crowd leaves. Great." He hung up and turned to me. "His training session just ended, so he agreed to meet us."

I stood up. "I know you've got things to do today. I'll just walk around town until we go to lunch."

"Not a good idea," he said. "Either the sheriff or his idiot nephew is sure to see you and hassle you in some way. There's a small office in the back that I fixed up in case I could ever afford a staff member. There's no phone but there's a good chair to sit in and a good desk to write on. Why don't you just hang out there until we go to lunch. In the meantime, I'll catch up on some work. Just keep your voice down, if you make a call."

He motioned toward the front where his aunt was still talking loudly to whomever had come in. I walked to the small office and sat down behind the desk. This would work well. I pulled out my cell phone and punched in a Portland number.

"Margot. Hi. It's Tom."

"Tom, it's good to hear your voice. Where are you?"

"I'm still in Burns."

"Any progress? Did you find out anything more about Mike?"

"Yeah, something important. Is Ned there?"

"Oh, Tom, that's wonderful. What did you find out?"

"Could you ask Ned to pick up another phone?"

I could hear her call to Ned who then came on the line.

"Hi Professor Martindale. How are you doing?"

"Are you two standing together?"

"Yes sir, we are."

"Ned, Tom found out something important."

"I don't know how to soft-pedal this, Margot. I found your husband's wallet."

"Oh, my God," she said.

"Margot, are you okay?" I asked.

"Tell me everything you know," she said. "I need to know everything."

I recounted the details of my walk into the canyon, the wild horses, and my discovery. "His driver's license was the first thing I noticed. Some money and his credit cards were still inside." I paused.

"Anything else? Are you holding something back?"

"There was what looked like dried blood on one corner of the wallet."

"God," said Ned. "Why him? My dad was a good man and always tried to do his best every day of his life. He didn't deserve this."

"I'm sorry," I said quietly. "That's all I have for now, but I'm working on a lot of angles out here."

"Thank you so much, Tom," said Margot. "We're counting on you."

I patted my pocket to make sure Mike Tateman's wallet was still there. I had tried to be as careful as possible with it, holding it by one corner while sliding it into my jacket. At Jeff's house, I had put it into a plastic bag to preserve any fingerprints that might still be usable.

* * * * *

The Cattlemen's Café was nearly empty when we walked in at about ten after one. The residents of this town did everything on a timetable and, apparently, noon to one was lunch time. Period.

"Sit anywhere you want, hon," said Dot, as she continued to clear tables in the front of the café.

Jeff led us to a booth about halfway back. Just as we slid in, Hank French arrived and sat down two tables away.

"Deputy French," said Jeff, in a voice loud enough for Dot and Diego, the cook, to hear. "Why don't you join us? I want you to meet someone."

French walked back and sat down next to Jeff and across from me.

"This is my old professor from college, Tom Martindale. Tom, this is a good friend of mine, Hank French. He's the chief deputy in the county."

The two of us shook hands.

"I'm impressed. We seldom have a genuine college professor out here in the sticks. So you taught this young squirt everything he knows. Too bad he forgot most of it before he took over the paper." French was smiling.

"Being a college professor is highly overrated, believe me, deputy. Lots of people hide behind their degrees and the arcane research they did to get them, when they really don't know how to deal with everyday life."

Dot showed up at this point, and we picked up our black-cornered menus to order. She looked at the three of us quizzically. "Didn't you all meet the other day?"

Deciding to ignore her astute observation, I said, "I'll have the taco plate."

"You want pintos or black beans with that, hon?"

"Pintos. Put the sour cream on the side, please. And iced tea with lemon to drink."

"You got it."

"Pintos?" smiled French. "You serving horse meat these days, Dot?"

"Oh, you wise guy." She punched him on the shoulder. "Always have to make a joke. I'm just gonna skip takin' your order if you keeping sassin' me."

She looked at Jeff.

"What about you, baby?"

"Same as my professor here."

"Even the pintos?"

Jeff nodded.

Dot turned to leave.

"How can I put an apology into words?" said French in mock horror. "I am so sorry to displease the best waitress this side of Boise. Or is it Bend?"

"Okay, you old turd. You win. What'll you have?"

"Same as my buddies."

As she turned to leave, French patted her arm. "I'd rather pat something else, and I would, if we were alone, but I don't want to embarrass our friends here with flamboyant displays of affection."

"You just keep your pats to yourself," said Dot, as she walked away smiling and loving every minute of this exchange.

Then French turned to me. "Okay, Tom. I'm ready to hear what this is all about."

I gave him a quick rundown on Mike Tateman's disappearance, the sheriff's inaction, and Margot's asking me to help.

"Doesn't surprise me at all," said French. "Sheriff Murchison and I disagree on most things so he keeps me out of the loop on a lot of the stuff that goes on. I keep the department running and the men trained, and he does the big, high-profile stuff. I gather from the urgency of Jeff's call that this has something to do with your friend's husband."

I pulled the plastic bag out of my pocket.

French glanced at it and put it into the pocket of his shirt. "Is this what I think it is?"

"Mike Tateman's driver's license is inside. There's a drop of something red on the corner."

"I hope you were careful."

I nodded.

"Where'd you find it?"

"Kiger Gorge."

"Not many people go in there, what with the horses and all. They get kind of frisky with outsiders."

"Yeah, didn't I find that out. A big stallion cornered me, so I climbed up into a small cave and that's where I found the wallet."

"That must have been Zebra. Biggest damn horse I've ever seen. How'd you happen to go in Kiger Gorge?"

"Some friends were with me at the hotel, and the wife found out from the manager that Mike Tateman had been asking about the horses and that canyon. The manager had given him a map."

"Who were your friends?"

"They're from Salem. My attorney and his investigator. They followed me up here and posed as married tourists. The trouble is, she's Black and he's Hispanic, so they couldn't actually work undercover."

French smiled and shook his head. "Yeah, we get pretty redneck when it comes to minorities around here. So this proves that your friend was in that canyon—and probably never left there, if you jump to the conclusion that no one would leave their wallet behind. In fact . . ."

"Here we are, gents. You too, Hank. The best tacos this side of . . ." she looked at French, "Boise."

"Thanks, my dear."

"You say that to all the girls, you old flirt. I'll be back when it looks like you're ready for pie. I've got to figure out my tickets for today so far."

"If your tips are big enough, you can take me to Vegas," said French.

Dot winked as she left us. Probably the greatest event in her life would be a romantic trip to Las Vegas with Hank French.

We enjoyed our food, which was again delicious. All three of us gave Diego a thumbs-up sign when he peeked out the pass-through window looking for our approval. He smiled.

"There's something else I didn't mention before," I said. I pulled out the Indian head penny and placed it on the table in front of the deputy.

French picked it up and turned it over. "Tateman's good luck piece?"

I nodded.

"You found it near the wallet?"

"No, I found it a few days ago on top of the mountain. That's how I knew Mike had been up there."

French frowned. "Look Tom, this is all well and good, I mean that you found these clues. But you just can't be poking around out here. You're an amateur, and amateurs can turn up injured or dead. We've probably got one body up there somewhere. We sure as hell don't want to wind up with another one." French handed the penny back to me. "Hang onto that for now. The wallet will suit our purposes. I'll get it analyzed at the state crime lab in Portland."

"How you gonna do that, with the sheriff breathing down your neck all the time?" asked Jeff.

"I'm gonna interest someone else in this case; he'll send it in, and the sheriff won't know about it. As soon as we finish eating, we're going to take a drive over to the courthouse. I've got some-one I want the two of you to meet."

CHAPTER 31

FRENCH PARKED IN FRONT OF THE COUNTY COURTHOUSE and motioned for the two of us to stay in the car.

"Before we go in, I want to tell you about the man you're going to meet," he said. "Russel Wright has been the D.A. forever. He'll never tell anyone his age, but he's got to be in his late 60s or early 70s. I can't remember when he was not the D.A. of this county. He keeps getting reelected because he is very good at what he does. Also, I doubt anyone else wants the job—it would be a career killer for anyone wanting to climb the legal career ladder. But there is another reason he's still the D.A.: he knows a lot about everyone in the county."

"Does that include the sheriff and Dickson White?" I asked hopefully.

"I have no doubt," said French. He glanced at me in the rearview mirror. "I don't know you, but Jeff vouches for you and I did some checking on my own, so I'm going to tell you some things that you can never repeat. If you do, I will deny it and I'll stop helping you find your friend. Agreed?"

"You have my word," I said. "I may be a former reporter—and you probably don't trust anyone in the media—but I will keep anything you tell me in strictest confidence."

"I believe you, Tom. You asked me if Russ Wright knows anything about the sheriff and Dickson White. He told me once that White foreclosed on his parent's failing farm, and it ruined them. They died soon after. I think Russ was away at law school at the time and couldn't do anything to help his family. To White, who was just starting his business at that time, the couple was just another impediment to getting what he wanted—extra land for his cattle operation. I guess he had bought their mortgage and just squeezed them out because he could. If I know Russ as well as I think I do, he'll listen to us today."

"That is harsh, and it sounds just like White. How about the sheriff?" asked Jeff.

"I suppose Wright finds him as unqualified for the job as I do and resents, as I do, the political clout White throws into each election to make sure Murchison gets reelected."

French opened the door and got out of the car. Jeff and I did the same. We walked up the steps and entered the courthouse. The sheriff led us up to the second floor, to one of those wood-paneled doors where the top half is frosted glass. The words "Russel H. Wright, County District Attorney" were painted on the glass.

We walked through the door and French said, "Hello, Thelma."

An older woman wearing horn-rimmed glasses looked up from her computer. She took off the glasses and let them dangle from the chain around her neck.

"Well, Hank French, as I live and breathe."

I didn't realize that people talked that way anymore, but we were in a part of Oregon that was, at times, unchanged from the way it had been thirty or forty years ago. I liked it. Her face showed genuine affection for the chief deputy, and I supposed that she had known him for years.

French hugged her and turned to us. "Thelma was my first grade teacher before she joined the district attorney's staff here. Always a pleasure to see you, Thelma."

"When am I going to get that invitation to your wedding?" she asked, winking at Jeff and me.

"I'm way past that ever happening," he said, blushing slightly. "My hours, the danger of the job . . ." His voice trailed off. "No one can take Janet's place. I just can't get it together to ever . . ."

Jeff and I exchanged glances, and I quickly changed the subject. "Thelma, this is a really nice old building. It's so well maintained."

"We try our best. It isn't easy, but we raise money here and there and get grants now and then. I'm glad you like it. It was built in 1940 for $63,000, replacing in the original one from 1890. Local folks raised most of the money after the WPA rejected a request for construction funds. They coughed up $4,000 to excavate a basement, but we didn't get the funds to have marble lobbies or elaborate Art Deco ornamentation on the building. We're proud of the artwork, though—all by local artists with cowboys, cattle roundups, and wildlife as the subjects. Heck, even the place where Hank's illustrious ancestor Pete French was killed is depicted in a picture in the clerk's office. The man who killed him, Edward Lee Olivier, was tried in 1898 in the old courthouse."

I found the history lesson interesting, but French was obviously tired of it. "Is his majesty receiving mere mortals today?"

"Let me go in and smooth the way," Thelma said smiling. "He's pretty grumpy today." She returned in a minute. "His mood has improved. Real lucky for the three of you. You can go right in."

French led the way into a huge room with high ceilings and tall windows overlooking the town. The room was filled with oak furniture: filing cabinets, stack bookshelves with glass doors, a roll-top desk, and a large table behind which Wright sat in a high-backed chair.

"May we approach the throne?" said French, a big smile on his face.

"You may proceed to be recognized," said the D.A. in a loud voice that was Shakespearean in tone and diction. He must have used it for years to bring juries to his side and frighten defendants and their attorneys. Wright stood up and extended his hand to Jeff and then to me. He was tall and thin, except for an ample belly which slipped out over a big silver belt buckle. His suit was rumpled and hung on him like it would on a scarecrow. His wide tie was stained, the knot askew and tied so that it did not quite reach the top button of his shirt.

"So, what brings you boys to my humble abode this fine afternoon?" he asked. "If you are here officially, Hank, it must mean you're bypassing our illustrious sheriff."

French started to answer, but the D.A. held up his hand.

"Save the explanation, dear Henry. I know you well enough to never question your presence in such circumstances." He turned to us. "I also know that our august chief deputy would not bring anyone in here that he did not trust to keep everything we say—no matter how dastardly or dire it may be—to ourselves."

Jeff and I shared a quick grin at the man's theatrical language and then nodded in agreement.

"If you do not, I will haul you into one of our lovely and well-restored courtrooms and cut off your balls, in a manner of speaking." Then he smiled as did French. A few seconds later, Jeff and I did so too, although a bit more tentatively. Wright waved us to a side area of his office where we sat down in chairs grouped around a low table.

Hank French then proceeded to give Wright the background about why we were there. When he needed details on Mike Tateman's disappearance, he turned to me.

"You know this Tateman well?" asked Wright.

"I never met him, but I know his wife and I trust her. I've known her since high school."

"And have you kept in touch with her over the years?"

"No, not at all. We've lived in Oregon about the same length of time, but we didn't know it."

Wright looked skeptical, but French broke into the conversation.

"If I can interject something here, Russ."

Wright waved his hand in assent. "By all means."

"I was a bit skeptical about this whole thing when Jeff first brought Tom to me for help, but from what Tom told me, the man who's lost, Michael Tateman, is a stellar guy, solid professional, good family man, etc. However, as soon as we're through here, I intend to run him through all the databases to double check that."

"Okay, okay. I'm almost convinced," said Wright. "And the sheriff didn't do much of anything to investigate this when the wife reported her husband missing?"

"Hardly lifted a finger," said French. "Told Tom he put his nephew Clay in charge. That is pretty laughable. I think you know me well enough to know that I wouldn't go outside of normal channels and bring this to you if I didn't believe the Sheriff's Office seriously screwed up. We need to make this right, Russ."

Wright waved his hand dismissively and turned to me. "You got something going on the side with your old high school flame?"

I didn't let my anger at his question show, but he was ticking me off with his brusque manner. I sighed and answered in a steady voice. "No sir. We served in a lot of student organizations and had some classes together in high school, but that was it. We lived on different sides of town—she in the north, more affluent side, me on the wrong side of the tracks, so to speak."

"Okay, okay. I get the picture," said Wright loudly. He put up his hands as a way to stop me. "Do you often go out on a limb like this to help your friends?"

"Yeah, I have been known to do that," I replied sheepishly.

French pulled out a sheet of paper from his pocket and glanced at it. "Tom here has been known to put himself in some jeopardy to help friends. He got a woman cleared of a murder charge on the coast a couple of years back and found the real killer. He brought a corrupt county sheriff to justice. He revealed a scheme to use illegal aliens as test subjects in some kind of dangerous research. In the process, he ran afoul of a Mexican drug gang."

French looked up as I felt my face turning red.

"Enough! Would you like to join my staff as an investigator?" Wright said to me, smiling. "Sometimes amateurs do a better job than the professionals, at least out here in the boonies. If we go forward with this investigation through this office, I have to tell you that I won't tolerate you going off on your own like you seem to have done in the past. You will help Hank French by providing information. Period. No heroics. No nighttime forays into the wilds of southeastern Oregon by yourself. If Hank needs you, he will ask for your help."

Then Wright turned to Jeff, who had remained silent throughout this exchange of words. "As for you, young ace, I do not want a word of any of this to get into your paper until I say it can. Understood?"

Jeff nodded. "Yes, sir."

"I've known you all your life, and I knew your parents. This town kind of raised you after they died. So I trust you. But don't get any kind of Pulitzer Prize-itis on this story. You'll have a humdinger of a story but not until I give the word!"

He turned to French. "Okay, what have we got, and what do you want to do?"

The chief deputy talked about my finding Tateman's wallet in the remote canyon and Dickson White's earlier threat to me to stay off his land. He mentioned the sheriff's nephew keeping an eye on me and the incident with the Arriagas at the old barn.

"Pretty thin stuff, Hank. None of this would make much of a case."

Wright turned to me. "When you went to the sheriff, he brushed you off about this Tateman's disappearance?"

"And Margot too, yes. That's Tateman's wife's name—my old friend."

"So you want to just nose around on your own, Hank?"

"I do, and I won't tell the sheriff."

"What do you want me to do?"

"I want you to know what I am doing and back me up legally when and if I find something. I don't want to get the goods on one or both of the Whites or the Murchisons and then have it all be swept under the rug. The sheriff's not a very good lawman but he has a powerful ally in White, and White has connections up the wazoo. I don't want my career to be ruined if I step on some toes."

"Agreed. I will protect you, but you need to keep me in the loop at all times. Every few days. Now, all of you get out of here so I can get some work done!"

CHAPTER 32

THE THREE OF US AGREED TO MEET AGAIN that night at Jeff's house to figure out what our next steps should be. French went to his office, Jeff to the paper, and I to Jeff's house. After making some coffee, I sat down to augment the chart I had constructed earlier about Mike Tateman's disappearance.

As I grabbed a legal pad to write my notes on, I remembered the notebook that Trina Hutchins had left at the hotel. I found it in a side pocket of my duffle bag. Trina's handwriting was easy to read because it looked like it had been done by a calligrapher.

The first half of the book contained notes about other cases she was working on for Lorenzo. I paged through them quickly because they were none of my business. About three-quarters into the small book, I found the beginning of the entries she had made in Frenchglen.

The first few pages covered things I already knew—how she and Lorenzo had arrived at the hotel posing as man and wife. How they had been insulted by the local redneck, my favorite law enforcement guy Clay Murchison. She recounted the trip up

Steens Mountain with the Grovers and Catherine Rickbone. The last entry made me spill my coffee.

June 23—This afternoon I went to have coffee in the dining room of the hotel. Sat down at a front table to look over the brochures in a rack. Lots of interesting things to do out here—especially for a city girl. Heard voices outside the window in the side yard, a woman and a man. At first, I paid no attention—none of my business. Voices grew louder. I peeked out. She was pretty and wore a waitress uniform. Guy was youngish, not bad looking but with what I call "mean eyes." No warmth.

He was rude when he talked. Said, "what the fuck do you want now" or words to that effect. She said she only wanted financial support for the boy. I presume a boy fathered by him that he did not acknowledge.

He said something like, "my dad won't let me pay a dime for the brat." She said, "you owe it to him," then "you owe it to us." He said, "I don't owe you a fuckin' thing" or something to that effect. She said, "if you don't give me what I want, I'll tell what I know about your dad's illegal horse business."

At that point, I ducked back out of sight because he glanced around and I was afraid he would see me. I heard him slap her hard and then scuffling as I guess he dragged her to his car. A minute after that, a car with a loud muffler peeled out. All I saw when I looked out was a cloud of dust.

I tossed the notebook on the table and finished my coffee. Why had Trina carelessly left the notebook behind and why hadn't she told me what she heard? I was mystified. She was a thorough investigator and it wasn't like her—or what I thought I knew about her—to be so careless. She and Lorenzo had left in a hurry but that was no excuse. Then it hit me: Trina had pulled out a book at our last meeting before she and Lorenzo left for Salem, but she had not opened it. She had told us what she found out—about Mike Tateman expressing interest in Kiger Gorge—but hadn't looked at her book. I paged back from the entries I had skipped earlier and there it was—an account of just that, Tateman asking Bates at the hotel about a map of the gorge area and about the wild horses. So she had just not remembered to tell me about the fight. And then later, when she was packing, I was willing to bet that Trina had confused the two books. What she thought she had taken with her was the book of her observations on the case. Instead, she had picked up the bird watching list Herb had given her to use on the mountain.

I punched Lorenzo's number on my cell phone and asked, "Is he in?"

"I am sorry, *señor*, but *Señor* Madrid is with a client. He is a very busy man, today and all days."

"I know, I know. I understand that. But he is my attorney too, and I need to speak with him on a matter that is *muy importante*."

"I am sorry, *señor*, but I have my orders."

"Will you do just one thing? Write my name on a slip of paper and place it in front of him."

"Very well, *señor*. I will do what you ask, but will you say a kind word for me to my boss if he becomes angry at me?"

"Yes, yes. Of course, I will do that."

"What is your name?"

"Oh, sorry. My name is Thomas Martindale."

"*Tomas* Martin . . . What is the rest of it? I did not get it."

"Tell him his friend Tom Martin is on the line, and I need to ask him a question."

Lorenzo picked up immediately. "Just a minute, Tom." He seemed to saying goodbye to someone in his office. "*Gracias. Hasta luego, señora.*" Then he spoke into the phone to me, "Sorry, I needed to say goodbye to my client. Okay, *Tomas Martine*. What do you desire of your humble servant, Lorenzo?"

"I know you're busy, so I won't go into much detail now. Things are moving along pretty fast. The chief deputy here is listening to me and has brought the local D.A. into the case."

"Is that Russel Wright?"

"Yeah. You know him?"

"Only by reputation. He spoke to my law school class once. He's a real character but an astute prosecutor. He knows everything there is to know about his county. Glad to hear he's helping you."

"I was calling about Trina."

"She's not here. I've got her working on that case I mentioned—about the substandard housing for migrant workers. She'll be checking in with me tomorrow. What's up?"

"It involves something she wrote in her notebook. You remember she was waving it at us the day you guys left? She didn't actually look at it but told us about Mike Tateman asking for directions to the Kiger Gorge area where the famous herd of mustangs live."

"Yes, I remember that."

"Well, I think Trina was really waving the bird book Herb Grover gave her to use on the mountain. She left her real notebook behind, and Bates at the hotel found and gave it to me. I just looked at it now and it's got the first real break we've had. Trina overheard a conversation between Junior White . . ."

"The son of the Mr. Big you think is involved in Tateman's disappearance?"

"Exactly. He was talking to the girl he got pregnant—that pretty waitress at the Cattlemen's Café. She was asking for child support and threatened to tell the world about some illegal activity in the gorge involving wild horses. The guy dragged her to the car and drove away in a hurry. That was two days ago. Trina didn't tell us about any of this."

"That surprises me. She's always very thorough. I'll ask her about it when she gets in tomorrow. Since she's undercover, we agreed not to talk unless she's in big trouble. She'll be exposed if anyone hears a cell phone ringing while she's working in the fields."

"She is really working in the fields? She mentioned it but I thought she was kidding."

"Yeah, she's posing as a Cuban woman on the run from the immigration people. If you haven't noticed, she loves playing roles. For this assignment, she's a cross between a Black Evita Peron and Eartha Kitt. So hang on for a day, and I'll get back to you."

"I can't wait that long, Lorenzo. White's ex-girlfriend might be in danger. I need to find out if she's missing and then figure out where she is."

"No, no, no, Tom. You promised me you wouldn't do that again. You know what happens when you play amateur detective."

"Look, Lorenzo, I've got Deputy French and my friend Jeff Walls to help me. I'll be fine. Sorry, Lorenzo. You're breaking up." I made static-like sounds into the cell phone over a line that was crystal clear. "You're fading, Lorenzo. Over and out."

Lorenzo was yelling at me when I disconnected.

CHAPTER 33

IT WAS LATE AFTERNOON when I arrived at Frenchglen. I had left messages for both Hank French and Jeff Walls when I was unable to reach them. I tried the Cattlemen's Café too, where I asked for Penny Brando. Dot, the loquacious waitress, said she hadn't been in to work for three days, and she was worried about her.

The parking lot of the hotel was empty, as were the porch and the dining room. Bates's assistant came out from the kitchen when she heard the front door close.

"We're fully booked up for tonight," she said, wiping her hands on a towel. "I might have something tomorrow night."

"I don't need a room. I was looking for Mr. Bates or a couple who I think are still staying here, the Grovers."

"The bird watchers. Yes, they're still staying here, but everybody went to Bend for the day. Some sort of bird exhibit at the High Desert Museum they were wanting to see. Mr. Bates had to go to John Day on business. Can I help?"

"No, not really. I just thought I'd go up the mountain and wanted company. Herb and Sue and their friend . . ."

"The tall, thin lady?"

"Yes. We went up there before."

"Oh yeah. I remember you. That was a couple of days ago. Didn't you stay with us a week or so back?"

"Yes, I did. One more question: do you know who Penny Brando is?"

"Of course, I do. That cute little waitress at the Cattlemen's. Got in trouble with that lout, Junior White. Boy, he's a piece of work. Won't do the right thing and marry her, and his daddy won't pay her a cent for that poor little boy's care. These rural girls, they make one mistake and open their drawers to a guy they think loves them and, bingo, they're pregnant and any plans they have for a future are out the window." She leaned closer to me and looked over her shoulder. "I think White and his whole bunch are up to no good, including that imbecile of a deputy, Clay Murchison. I don't care if he is the sheriff's nephew. That doesn't give him the right to come in here and insult our customers and strut around like he owns the world."

"I saw that myself a couple of times with the Grovers and another couple, a Hispanic man and his African American wife."

"Yeah, I remember you were here when that happened. Very embarrassing."

"Back to Penny Brando . . . have you seen her out here in the past few days?"

The woman shook her head. "Not lately. One afternoon last week, I think on my day off, I was going to take a nap. I live in that tiny trailer on the edge of the property. Anyways, I heard these loud voices, and when I peeked out I saw Penny and that good-for-nothing Junior White arguing right outside my window."

"Did you see what happened? Did they leave together?"

"I don't like to get involved in domestic stuff like that. I pulled the blinds and turned on my TV—loud."

"Well, no one's seen Penny for the past few days, so I came to see if anyone out here had."

"You want to see her, I gather." The woman was looking at me quizzically, then her eyes narrowed. Why did a stranger want to find a young waitress?

I thought fast. "I'm a college teacher and one of my former students, Jeff Walls, said he thought Penny might be interested in going to college. I was just following up on that."

Her face immediately relaxed. "That's nice of you. Boy, Penny could certainly use some help."

I turned to leave. "Nice talking to you."

"Can I give you a cup of coffee and a piece of pie, maybe?"

"No, thanks. I'd better be going. I think I'll drive up the mountain one last time before I leave to go back to the valley."

"Should be a pretty sunset tonight," she said. "It'll get cooler too as you drive up the mountain. Pretty much of a scorcher today." She wiped her brow with the towel.

"I'll see you around."

"Not if I see you first." Then she laughed at her little joke and walked back into the kitchen.

* * * * *

An hour later, near the top of the mountain, I pulled off into a parking area and drove to the far end behind some stumpy trees. I had brought water and a hat. At the last minute, I grabbed a sweatshirt out of the backseat and tied it around my waist by the sleeves. Although I didn't need it now, it might be colder in the shady canyon I was heading for.

The walk down into Kiger Gorge was easy, although I had to be careful that I didn't trip over large rocks here and there along the way. The unwary hiker—like me—might easily fall in the uneven terrain.

As before, I reached the bottom quickly and headed into the canyon itself. I passed the ledge where I had escaped the stallion and pushed on. The canyon was deeper than I thought. I was surprised that the horses were nowhere in sight, but as I walked a bit farther I saw the stallion, mares, and two foals grazing several hundred yards away. I walked back to the ledge and climbed up. I pulled out my water bottle and took a long swig. So far, the stallion had not sensed my presence. If something was going to happen here involving the horses, it would happen after the sun went down. I closed my eyes.

When I awoke several hours later, it was dark and a bit chilly. The sky was clear and a full moon cast an eerie light on the canyon. I pulled the sweatshirt over my head and drank some water. The horses were still in place. I looked up at the sky and marveled to myself at the abundance of stars. You sure couldn't see that many stars in the city with all the other lights around.

As I contemplated the nocturnal beauty, I heard the distant rumble of several trucks. The stallion heard it too and came to attention, whinnying loudly. The mares and foals began to run around him, seeking protection. The stallion ran toward the sound, then stopped just opposite my resting place.

Just then, three pickups pulling trailers drove into view, their movements slowed by the uneven terrain. They stopped near to where I was hiding and five men jumped out. Behind them, Dickson White's yellow Hummer stopped too and three men got out: Junior White, Marty, and Clay.

The group walked to one side of the truck and White nodded to the men. At his signal, they unloaded long sections of fencing and then set it up into a corral.

Until now, the horses had remained still. The stallion seemed not to move a muscle as he guarded his brood. He whinnied once and everyone looked at him. Then he reared up and led all the horses in the other direction.

The horses ran around and around the canyon, but they were trapped by the men and their vehicles. The stallion stopped and, at his signal, the other horses clustered behind him, as if for protection.

White nodded to his men, and they unloaded their own horses from the trailers, mounted them, and began to advance on the wild mustangs from opposite sides. As they got near the stallion, one began to swing his lasso and then hurled the loop at the big horse. He dodged it easily, but two of the mares were not so lucky. The men snared them with their ropes and led them into the makeshift corral. Two of their foals followed quickly.

The stallion was very unhappy at this turn of events and charged the men on horseback. They deflected his advance easily, and he paused to repeat his action.

"DON'T HURT THE STALLION!" yelled White. "WE NEED HIM FOR MR. FUAD!"

I felt helpless to do anything about what was happening. What chance did I have against all these men? White and the others would probably kill me if they knew I had discovered their horse rustling operation.

Just then, my worries were compounded as I looked to my left and saw the biggest snake I have ever seen, rattling loudly and poised to strike.

CHAPTER 34

I LET OUT A STARTLED YELP but managed to pinch it off quickly. Unfortunately the horses and the men heard it. Before the men could react, the stallion galloped to the enclosure and lunged at the wires of the corral as if he was trying to tear it down. He bellowed and pranced for several minutes before galloping away. The mares whinnied as he fled.

"DON'T SHOOT!" screamed White. "HE'S NO GOOD TO US DEAD!"

The snake had stopped rattling but had not moved from its perch. It began to sway back and forth. That delay allowed me to inch away slowly. I easily slid into the entrance of a cave on the hillside. I kept moving as the snake kept swaying, and I was soon obscured in the shadowy front entrance. From here, I could watch both the snake and the men below without being seen.

White's befuddlement over losing the stallion only lasted a minute, and he was soon issuing orders again. He waved his arms and whistled to bring all the men in close. Soon, several of them loaded the wild horses into a trailer, while the others dismantled the portable corral and slid its pieces into the truck. Then he yelled for the men to stop their work on the corral. The sudden quiet and the high canyon walls made any sound reverberate as clearly as if it was being amplified by a loud speaker.

He pulled one of the men away from the others and pointed toward where I was hiding. "Find out what the hell happened that caused the horses to react like they did. I think I heard something up there on that ledge."

The man loped toward me, and I saw that it was Marty, the cowboy who had been in the hotel the first night I stayed there and in the barn with Junior. While he climbed up the incline, I scooted farther back into the cave, which was larger than it looked.

As soon as he hoisted himself up onto the ledge, he saw the snake. Seeing a new victim, the snake began to shake its rattle again and raise its head, ready to strike. Marty pulled out a revolver and shot the snake's head off. The head flew high in the air and landed near the opening, then it rolled toward me, the fangs still sticking out. Marty picked up the body and waved it in the air, the sudden movement causing the rattle to ring out.

"IT WAS A SNAKE, A GODDAMNED RATTLESNAKE!"

Then he raised the body over his head and swung it around and around as if it were a lasso. When he released it, the snake went sailing off like a kite tail in the wind. Marty turned and jumped down from the ledge and ran over to where the others were standing. The men gathered around him and patted him on the back, except for Junior White who stood next to this father.

For his part, White Senior could stand this idleness no longer. "I'm not paying you all this money to lollygag out here. Let's move out and get back to work."

Some of the men got into the trucks and others mounted their horses, and the whole caravan moved slowly out of the canyon, led by White's Hummer. The dust from the truck tires and the horses' hooves was visible in the headlights of the vehicles.

I breathed a sigh of relief at my narrow escape. As I sat back to rest, a strong smell filled my nostrils—an odor that was not familiar but whose pungency made me gag. Apparently, the wind had shifted because I had not smelled it at first. I hadn't realized how large the cave was because it was L-shaped. I stepped into the other chamber, where something caught my eye on the opposite side of the cave: a dusty boot.

I hesitated, then walked over to it. Next to the boot was another one, half buried in the dust. Both boots were attached to legs and my gaze drifted up to see the torso of a man, dressed in hiking gear and leaning against the cave wall as if at rest, a cap on his head. As I moved closer, I could see the logo on the front of the cap: Northwestern University Law School.

CHAPTER 35

"MY GOD," SAID JEFF. "What a grisly sight! Are you in shock?" He handed me a shot glass full of whiskey, which I drank fast.

I had called both Jeff and the chief deputy as soon as I got back to town. We met at Jeff's house.

"No, I don't think so. I saw dead people from time to time in my reporting days. I guess it was the realization that it was Mike Tateman that affected me the most. Like what I came out here to accomplish turned out so badly."

"You had to expect something like that," said French. "A guy doesn't go missing for weeks up there and then walk into the Frenchglen Hotel in time for dinner. You said that yourself."

"Yeah, you're right." I took another swig of the whiskey.

"So, you say Dickson White, Junior White, the sheriff's nephew, and a bunch of ranch hands were out there to round up the horses?" French asked.

I nodded. "They seemed especially interested in the stallion. White talked about a Mr. Fuad."

"I'm going to go out on a limb here and say that White has been rounding up the Kiger mustangs and selling them to customers from overseas. It's pretty obvious that it's an Arab, I mean, with the name you mentioned," said French.

"What would be so special about the stallion?" asked Jeff.

"Foreign buyers would want him for his sperm—to breed with their own mares and strengthen the bloodline of their horses," said French. "Arabs love horse racing and owning their own race horses. Because the bloodline of these horses goes so far back, and has been kept pure, they would be in great demand."

"And White, with all his arrogance, decides he does not have to follow the same rules as everyone else and sells the horses to someone from abroad," I said.

"And I'll bet Mike Tateman stumbled onto his operation," said French. "That's probably what got him killed."

Jeff and I nodded our heads in agreement.

"So, what do we do?" I asked.

"*You* don't do anything but show me where the body is," said French. "I'm trying to ignore the fact that you did what I told you not to do. This is a police matter and also a federal matter because the BLM is involved. The horses are their property. They have a mandate to protect them."

I shrugged my shoulders. French thought for a moment.

"Okay, here's what we're going to do."

* * * * *

On finding that both the sheriff and his nephew were taking a sick day, French acted under his authority as chief deputy to round up the other six men in the department and tell them to be ready to handle a crime scene. He did not tell them where they were going or what they would find when they got there. He told them not to tell anyone what they were doing, including the sheriff. He told us that he was relying on the fact that most, if not all, of the men disliked the sheriff and his nephew and would not miss their participation.

While they assembled their gear, French and I went over to the courthouse to meet with Russel Wright. The D.A. had been asleep at home when the deputy called but met with us at his office a half-hour later. He called in his secretary to take down my statement about what I had seen and where I had seen it.

Based on my statement alone, Wright had sanctioned a full investigation. Even though French could have gone out there on his own, any later case would be strengthened by the D.A.'s involvement at this early stage. His curiosity aroused, Wright had grabbed his battered hat and followed us out the door, growling to his assistant, "You finish up this statement, Thelma, and then go home. You don't have to come in until noon tomorrow."

* * * * *

It took us over two hours to get to Kiger Gorge and drive in to where I had found the body. It was almost dark. The deputies got out of several pickups and began to unload a generator. Soon, strong lights flooded the area. I directed one of the deputies to train a beam to the left toward the cave. I walked over to the ledge and climbed up on it, French following closely behind me. I pointed to the body and quickly turned away—the stench was so strong it made me gag. French knelt down and shined his light up and down the torso but he did not touch it. He turned toward the men who had gathered at the base of the ledge.

"Dennis, I want crime scene tape strung out in about a 200-foot half circle," he said to one man, "from over there to over here. Steve, climb up here with your camera and take as many shots of the body as you need from all angles. But don't move it." He looked at the others. "Better put on face masks. The smell is pretty bad up here. It won't kill you, but it'll sure make you feel sick."

He turned to me and tossed me a mask. "Right, Tom?"

One of the men handed masks to Wright and Jeff. French had allowed Jeff to come along because of his earlier promise to give him an exclusive on this story. Jeff helped Wright up onto the ledge, and they ventured into the cave. The smell drove them out after a few minutes.

French jumped down from the ledge, and I followed.

"Okay, I want you men to move out another hundred yards or so and start an intensive ground search," French said. "I know it's dark and I know it's cold, but you've got to do this anyway. We'll do it again in the morning, but we've lost a lot of valuable time in this case already, so I want to do a search now."

The men fanned out and searched the ground, guided by strong flashlights and the beams of the several searchlights which one of the men maneuvered as needed.

French motioned us back to his car. "Let's us four get inside and talk for a bit," he said.

We got in and Jeff passed around a flask. Everyone but French took a swig. In fact, Wright took five swigs, smacking his lips after each one. He wiped his mouth with his sleeve when he was finished and shook the flask, which seemed empty. He shrugged and handed it back to Jeff.

French picked up the microphone from his radio and got the dispatcher on the line. "Shirley, I want you to patch me through to Doc Natali. I know it's late, but I need to speak with him."

French waited impatiently for a few minutes, then the doctor apparently came on the line, along with a lot of static.

"Doc, I need you to come out to Kiger Gorge as fast as you can. KIGER GORGE. I'm investigating a homicide, and I can't move the body until you take a look at it. A BODY! A DEAD BODY! Okay, we'll be waiting." French turned to the three of us. "Doc is pretty hard of hearing, but he'll be here as soon as his old bones can do it."

Wright looked at me. "Doc is our medical examiner. He's old but he's good. As soon as he looks things over and releases the body, we'll take your poor friend out of there and move him to Portland. It's standard procedure for us to send our bodies to the Oregon State Medical Examiner. It takes more time, but those people will be able to give us good information—condition of the body, wounds, how long it's been here, maybe even cause of death. Things like that."

While we waited for the doctor to arrive, we sat quietly and watched the men as they searched the area. Because I had pointed out the spot where the corral had been set up, they avoided that for now.

In about an hour, French sent one of his men in an all-terrain vehicle to meet the doctor up on the road at the entrance to the canyon. A half-hour later we heard the ATV and a car thumping along the ruts into the gorge.

The four of us got out, and French and Wright walked over to greet the doctor. He got out of the pickup slowly and took some time to straighten up and walk over to us. I noticed that he had a slight limp.

"Don't ever get old," he said. Then he looked at Wright. "But, hell, Russel, you ARE old!" Then he threw his head back and laughed heartily. French smiled, but Wright glared at the old man.

Dr. Natali looked like a country doctor in a Swedish film. He was tall and thin and had a full head of gray hair and a huge mustache. His wire-rimmed glasses were perched so low on his nose that they looked like they might fall off, but they gave him a studious appearance.

"Thanks for coming out, doc," said French. He introduced us.

"You I don't know, but I brought this young fellow into the world," he said, as he passed me quickly and stood in front of Jeff. "You know, your parents were two of the best people I've ever met. I'm so sorry for your loss."

Jeff took a deep breath and then shook the doctor's hand. "Thank you, sir. I appreciate that."

Natali looked at the young deputy who had driven him up here. "Would you be kind enough to fetch my bag, deputy?"

The deputy walked to the truck and pulled out the bag, which he started to hand to the doctor.

"I'll haul that for you, doc," said French, taking the large bag from the deputy.

"Thanks, son. You can take me to the body now."

Jeff and I stayed where we were as French, Wright, and the doctor walked over to the cave. The young deputy followed them. When they got to the ledge, French nodded to the younger man and then the two of them put their hands together. The doctor put one foot and then the other into this makeshift step and the other two hoisted him up onto the ledge. French followed him quickly, and they disappeared inside the cave.

In ten minutes or so, they reappeared. French jumped down and looked up at the doctor. This time, Natali stepped down from the ledge on his own, stripping off a face mask and rubber gloves as he descended.

"Nasty things, bodies. We live in them for years and years and get used to their various peculiarities. We pamper them when we're younger and coax them into hanging together when we're older. But when they die on us, they turn into vile objects that nobody wants to look at or deal with." He glanced at the four of us. "It's hard for me to say much about the cause of death at this point. Since it's summer, it's been real hot out here for weeks. The high heat of the days would speed decomposition. That's what the bad smell is from—the leaking of body fluids. Lividity has come and gone." Natali pointed toward the cave. "Let's get that poor fellow out of there."

French nodded to a group of deputies who were standing nearby and they walked to the cave, one of them unfurling a body bag. They climbed onto the ledge and disappeared inside the cave. In five minutes, they reappeared with the bulky bag and carefully lowered it over the side of the ledge to the other men waiting below.

French walked to his four-wheel-drive vehicle and rearranged the rear seats to form a flat area. "Slide him in here," he said to his men. "Carefully. He's suffered enough indignity already." He looked at the doctor. "You okay to get our guy back to Burns? I'll radio the state police to meet you at your office and transfer the body to Portland."

"Fine, fine. I'm happy to do it," he said. He walked over to us and shook our hands. "It's been a pleasure to work with you." Then the doctor turned and limped to the vehicle. He waved at us as he disappeared from view.

"Great man," Jeff muttered.

"Yes, there's no one quite like the doc," said French.

"He's a legend," said Wright, with a growl and then under his breath, "in his own mind."

French patted him on the back. "Why Russ, I do believe you're jealous. You know, we do have room out here for more than one curmudgeon. It's a big country."

CHAPTER 36

I WOKE UP TO SHOUTS THE NEXT MORNING. It was ten thirty. I had only been in bed for a few hours.

"MARTINGALE. I KNOW YOU'RE IN THERE! SHOW YOURSELF!"

I slipped on some jeans and a T-shirt and shoes, walked down the stairs, and moved the blind. Clay Murchison was standing on the porch of Jeff's house. I opened the door, and he pushed me aside and stepped into the living room.

"You got a warrant, deputy?"

"You don't need a warrant when your uncle's the sheriff!"

"What am I being charged with?"

"Tampering with evidence and defiling a corpse."

Clay made a cursory look into all of the rooms on the main floor. So far, he had not drawn his gun.

"Ever hear of *habeas corpus*, sheriff?"

"Habeas what? Don't spout your fancy words at me. Git some clothes on. We're going downtown. We'll see how you like the inside of our nice jail."

I sat down on the sofa.

"I'm not going anywhere until you tell me what I'm being charged with." I folded my arms across my chest.

"What the hell?" Jeff had opened the door and stood there. "What's going on? Tom? Clay?"

"Deputy Murchison, you punk," Clay replied snidely.

"Have you gone crazy, Clay? What do you think you're doing? This man is a respectable college professor and my guest. You have no right to barge in here and accost him. Does your uncle know about this?"

"No, but he soon will. He'll agree with me. This man's a suspect in the death of a man out in Kiger Gorge."

"A suspect? He found the body, you idiot!"

Clay walked over to Jeff and hit him hard with the handle of his gun. Jeff slumped to the floor. I started to get up to see if I could help him, but Clay shoved me down. Jeff wasn't moving, and I silently cursed myself for dragging him into this.

"Stand up and turn around," Clay said.

"You just shoved me down. Now you want me to stand up?"

"I'm warning you," yelled Clay. "Just shut the fuck up and do what I say."

I stood up and soon felt handcuffs sliding onto my wrists from behind, very tight handcuffs.

"Okay, we're getting out of here. Walk ahead of me and don't try anything."

When we got to his car, Clay put a black hood over my head and shoved me onto the rear floor. He got in, started the car, and sped away so fast that I hit my head on the underside of the front seat. We drove for what seemed like a long time, and then he stopped.

"I'm here. At the old barn. Where are you? . . . Yeah, I got the bastard. . . . Get here as fast as you can. I don't know what to do now. . . . You're the mastermind. You'll figure it out!"

Clay got out of the car and opened the rear door. He pulled on my feet and dragged me toward him. My face hit the hump in the floor.

"Ouch!" I yelled.

"Shut up and stand up."

I did what he said and felt a bit dizzy because I couldn't see my surroundings. "Could you at least take off the hood? My face is on fire."

Clay jerked off the hood, and I blinked at the strong sunlight. My face felt like it was bleeding. "I'm hurt. I need a doctor. I feel blood all over my face!"

"You'll live," he said, starting to hand me a handkerchief.

"I can't very well treat my wound with my hands tied behind me."

He grunted and unlocked the cuffs. Then he pulled my arms forward and placed the handcuffs on me again. He started laughing and shoved me ahead of him into the barn where Lorenzo and I had met his Basque friends and encountered Junior White several weeks before.

I sat down on a bale of hay and faced him. "You know that you're in a lot of trouble, don't you? I don't know if you had anything to do with the death of my friend, but you sure as hell know who did. Was it your friend Junior White? Or his father, the great Dickson White?"

"Shut the fuck up," yelled Clay, running his hands over his face. "I've got to think."

"I guess you do, deputy. Why do you want to risk everything for a punk who has probably used you all your life?" I figured I had nothing to lose by ratcheting up the rhetoric. Or so I thought.

"You gonna let this prick talk to you that way, Clay?" Junior White stepped into the barn.

"So, Mr. Big has arrived," I said. "We can all take a deep breath and rejoice."

Junior White walked over to me and slapped me hard. The blow did nothing for my bruised face, which began to throb. "Oh, sorry," he snarled. "Did I hurt your ow-ie?" He turned to Clay. "So, what does he know about what happened?"

Clay looked sheepish. "Well . . . I . . . was waiting for you, Junior. You know how to do this kind of stuff better than me."

"That figures, Clay. You always were a bit slow in the head." White pointed to his head and crossed his eyes.

"You shouldn't talk that way about your oldest friend." We all turned to see Penny Brando stepping into the barn.

"Penny. What the hell are you doing here?" asked White. "Shouldn't you be taking care of that brat of yours or waiting tables at the Cattlemen's? That's the only job sluts like you can get in this one-horse town."

Penny squared her shoulders and faced White with a defiant look on her face. "If I'm a slut, you made me one. I should have listened to my friends back then and kept as far away from you as I could. In fact, I tried to hitch a ride to Eugene in hopes that I could earn enough money to get away from you forever.

"You know you wanted it," shouted White, fondling his crotch. "You wanted it big time!"

"And all I got for that one night was a world of hurt. And you know what?" She turned to Clay and me. "It wasn't all that great! Junior here's got a pretty tiny pecker!"

White let out a roar and grabbed Penny by the shoulders. He shook her, and then hit her jaw hard. She fell to the floor.

"Junior, you ought not to have done that," said Clay, meekly. "She might be hurt bad."

"Yeah, big man picking on young women," I yelled. "Must feel great. Did that little pecker come alive?"

White walked over to me and raised his hand to hit me, then stopped.

"No, I won't do that. I won't kill you here. I've got other plans for you. Big plans. I'm not ready to send you to the big classroom in the sky just yet."

CHAPTER 37

IT WASN'T ENTIRELY CLEAR TO ME why White took us to Kiger Gorge. I couldn't figure out why the "other plans" he had for me couldn't be carried out in any isolated place. God knows, almost everywhere out here could have that designation.

White had borrowed his father's Hummer, and he shoved me in the rear compartment. He took off the handcuffs, then tied my wrists behind me with the same rope looped around my ankles. This way, he could make me very uncomfortable with a quick tug. Lying with my face touching the floorboard, I could barely move. Although I could not see her, Penny was probably in the seat in front of me, with Clay sitting in the front with Junior.

It was midafternoon by this time, but it sounded like there was little traffic on the highway to the Steens. The sky was getting dark with hints that a thunderstorm might be heading our way. After a few miles, I could hear its distant rumble and see flashes of lightning reflected on the windows of the vehicle.

After about a half-hour, we started down the rocky surface that led to the canyon. Reckless by nature, Junior White did not let the uneven surface slow him down. If anything, he drove faster.

"Easy Junior," yelled Clay. "You're gonna wreck your dad's Hummer."

"Shut the fuck up," said Junior. "He'll just buy me another one."

Spoken like a true, spoiled rich kid.

The sun had broken through the clouds as we drove into the gorge itself. While I couldn't tell exactly where we were, I caught a glimpse of the high walls I had seen the day before. After a few more minutes of going up and down the various ruts, White stopped the car. He opened the door and walked back to the rear, then opened the hatch and yanked on the rope.

"Up, up, up! Get your sorry ass out of there."

"If you want me to walk, you're going to have to loosen this rope," I shouted.

White got out a knife and cut the rope that extended down my back. That freed my feet, and I was able to stand up. My hands were still tied behind me, but I felt a bit more comfortable.

Clay had pulled Penny out of the rear seat and was standing nearby, holding her in his arms. "Why'd you hit her so hard, Junior?" he said. "She's still out cold."

"That bitch deserves whatever I do to her," he snarled.

"Big man, knocking out a defenseless woman," I said. "That takes a really big man."

Surprisingly, White ignored my taunts and looked back toward the entrance of the canyon. Soon I heard the sound of engines and the crunch of tires on the rocky ground. When the dust cleared, a number of vehicles came into view: another Hummer, a big SUV, and three pickups pulling horse trailers.

Junior tied me to the door handle of the Hummer and walked over to the men who emerged from the other vehicles.

"Hi, Dad," he said to his father, who met him halfway.

The elder White ignored his son's hand and hit him hard across the face with a whip.

"Oww! Why'd you do that for?"

"For your general stupidity over the years and for bringing this guy Martingale out here. And Penny too. What were you thinking?"

"I thought . . ."

"Now wouldn't THAT be a novel concept—you thinking."

The senior White walked over to me. "I knew you would cause trouble the first time I saw you on my land. Why'd you have to stick your goddamned nose in something that doesn't concern you?"

"Oh, but it does concern me," I said, putting my face as close to White as I could manage with my arms tied to the vehicle. "You had my friend killed. What happened? Did he discover your little horse rustling operation here? What's it all about? Are you selling horses to Arabs?"

White looked surprised. "How'd you know that? Did one of these knuckleheads tell you?"

I smiled at his discomfort. "Let's just say that a little bird told me. I think it was one of those buzzards who swoop around up here. That sure seems appropriate, given the way you and your son operate."

Now it was White Senior's turn to hit me. Fortunately, he used his hand and not his gun. My white skin was rapidly turning black and blue.

White walked to the rear of the black SUV and opened the door. A large, beefy man got out. He was holding a rifle and quickly scanned the tops of the canyon walls before shoving White aside and extending his hand to someone in the car.

A small man wearing an expensive-looking suit and a white burnoose got out. The headgear was held in place with gold braid. White walked over to him and shook his hand vigorously. Then he raised his arm and two of his men walked around to the side of the semi trailer and slid open the doors. They pulled a ramp up to the door and then led two beautiful mares and their foals down to the ground. Both mares were wearing halters.

"Bring them over here," White said. "We need to let the big fellow see them."

The wranglers led the horses to the area where the corral had been set up earlier. The horses began to dance around in anticipation and whinny loudly.

All of a sudden, the big stallion appeared at the other end of the canyon, leading a line of horses. He galloped toward the mares, then stopped abruptly, dust flying in every direction.

Beyond White, the man in the expensive suit and white burnoose moved closer to the corral, his beefy bodyguard standing nearby with his rifle at the ready. We all stared at the huge horse, transfixed by his beauty. His eyes sparkled and his coat shined as he began to prance back and forth as if at a horse show. Although I know little about horses, I was sure that this one was the best of his breed. I could easily see why this Arab coveted him.

"I guess you're going to get even richer than you already are by selling this horse to your friend with the burnoose," I said to White. "He needs some new blood in his racing stable?"

"Shut up, Martingale. This doesn't concern you."

The horse continued to dance, and we continued to stare at him. Then, at White's signal, his men led the mares closer to the stallion so that they were nose-to-nose with him. They all whinnied, and one of the cowboys handed the reins to his partner. I saw that it was Marty, the cowboy I had first met at the Frenchglen Hotel and who had killed the rattlesnake. He pulled a lasso out of his belt and slowly advanced toward the stallion.

Marty moved the rope over the head of the giant horse in a swift motion that seemed to catch him off guard. The stallion tried to rear up but Marty held him down—a difficult task because of his great strength.

"DICKSON WHITE, STEP AWAY FROM THE VEHICLE AND PUT YOUR HANDS IN THE AIR!" said a voice that reverberated off the sides of the gorge. "YOU ARE SURROUNDED!"

White looked surprised and confused. The noise caused Marty to turn away from the stallion and loosen his grip on the rope. That was all the great horse needed. He reared up and came down hard on the head of the cowboy who was holding the other horses. The cowboy screamed in pain and slumped to the ground.

Now free of their restraints, the mares raced easily away with the stallion, the foals following closely behind. The dust created by their hooves quickly obscured them as they vanished back into the far reaches of the canyon.

Five vehicles drove into the canyon and men jumped out of them. I could see uniforms of the Oregon State Police, as well as the Sheriff's Department and the BLM.

"Are you okay, Tom?" Jeff Walls ran to my side and quickly untied me.

"I'm fine, but you don't look all that great."

A bandage covered one side of his face.

"I got pretty banged up when Clay hit me," he said, rubbing his face. "Took some stitches to stop the bleeding."

I looked over at Penny. In the melee, Clay had placed her so she was leaning against the car. Her eyes were open, but she looked a bit dazed. Clay had not put up a fight and was following a state policeman meekly to one of the vehicles.

"Is there a medic?" I shouted. "This girl needs help."

A woman wearing a flack jacket quickly ran over and knelt down. She pulled something from her bag and put it under Penny's nose.

Behind them, I saw two of the state troopers disarming the bodyguard and helping the Arab into a patrol car.

"I can't leave you alone for a minute," said French, who had walked up. "Do you always get into this much trouble?"

"I don't know what you're talking about," I said with a smile.

CHAPTER 38

"DO YOU ENJOY A GOOD SMOKE, Mr. Martindale?"

"No, can't say that I do."

Russel Wright was holding court in his office the next morning. Hank French, Jeff Walls, Lorenzo Madrid, and I were sitting around his massive desk, hanging on his every word—just the way he liked it, I'm sure.

I had asked Wright's permission to bring Lorenzo into the meeting after he arrived in Burns to check on my welfare. I didn't think I needed an attorney because of anything I had done. Given Dickson White's irrationality, however, I couldn't be certain. He seemed like the type of person who would sue you just out of meanness or as a way to deflect attention from his own problems.

Wright opened the humidor on his desk and passed it around.

"They're Perdomo's. You may be accustomed to the ones from Cuba, Mr. Madrid."

"No, I can't say I've ever had the pleasure."

"Good thing they're not illegal, Russel," said French. "I'd have to haul you in for dealing in contraband."

Wright smiled and leaned back in his chair, his feet on his desk. French, Lorenzo, and Wright lit their cigars and puffed on them for several minutes, large smoke rings rising in the air.

"This is looking like a commercial for cigar *aficionados*," I said. "I'd like to hear what's going to happen in this case. I need to call Margot and fill her in."

"Hold your horses—no pun intended," said Wright. "You city people are always in too much of a hurry." He puffed some more, then sat upright in his chair, his hands on the desk. He glanced at some papers in front of him. "Okay, here's the scoop. First, on your friend, Mr. Tateman. His skull had a bullet hole in it, so obviously that's what killed him. As they were turning the body at one point, a cartridge fell on the floor. Also, the medical examiner said that the body showed signs of trauma. Lots of bruising all over, like he had been beaten up. Both hands were broken, like he'd been in a fight. And these were fresh breaks, not ones that happened in the past. But he didn't die from a beating. Also, there were hair particles on his clothing. The DNA did not match his own hair. The hair was red. Mr. Tateman had brown hair."

"Sounds like White or his son," said French. "Both of them have red hair, although the father's hair has mostly gone to gray."

"Bingo," said Wright. "We're getting hair samples from the Whites today, as soon as I can get a court order. Both of them have lawyered up big time.

"As for the bullet, I've impounded everyone's gun—Dickson White, Junior White, Deputy Clay—and had them tested. They're all .45s, which is what most ranch hands use. But the bullet does not match any of their guns."

"Will we ever know who killed Mike Tateman?" I asked.

"Your guess is as good as mine at this point," said Wright. "It has to be one of three people: Dickson White, Junior White, or

Deputy Clay. As to motive, I'd imagine that your friend stumbled onto the horse rustling operation when he was hiking in Kiger Gorge and someone panicked. Hank here will get it out of Junior eventually. Right, Hank?"

The chief deputy nodded. "I'll get out the thumbscrews. It may take a while because he doesn't make a move without his daddy's okay, but he'll crack in time. Basically, he's a coward, but I think he'll tell everything he knows to save himself from death row."

"Is the sheriff involved in this?" I asked.

"Not so far as I can prove," said Wright. "He'd have to be aware of some of it and his nephew, that idiot Clay, is like Junior White. He doesn't take a shit without his uncle's okay."

"What about the Arab man I've been hearing about?" asked Lorenzo. "Tom said he was the customer. What happened to him?"

Wright said he found out that Mr. Fuad has diplomatic immunity. "He's from one of those tiny countries on the Arabian Peninsula where the ruler is obsessed with raising race horses. He wants to create a new breed by combining the blood of that stallion with his own Arabian ponies. But he did not break the law, at least not technically. He was not in this country illegally, and he has the run of the continental U.S. because of his status. Hell, even the bodyguard had a permit to carry that big gun of his. Both of them are free and are probably on their way back to the Middle East as we speak."

"What about Penny Brando?"

"She's going to be all right." Jeff, not Wright, answered my question, his face turning red.

"So, are you and Penny about to become an item?" I asked.

He blushed again. "Well, yeah, I guess. She's a fine girl who just got off on the wrong foot in life by being seduced by the big, handsome football player."

"Happens all the time out here," said Wright, a sad look on his face. "You gonna make an honest woman of her?"

"Yeah, I'm going to try."

Wright turned to me. "Mr. Tateman's body can be released as soon as the examination is complete. Then I'll sign the release and give the order."

"I'll call Margot right now and tell her the news. I've been waiting for the right time."

* * * * *

Margot answered after four rings. Lorenzo and I were at Jeff's house, getting ready to leave for the valley.

"Margot. Hi, it's Tom. Are you sitting down?"

"Yes, Tom, I am. Ned's here with me. Do you have some news?"

"Yes, I do. We found Mike's body yesterday."

"Oh God, I've waited for this moment for so long. Tell me about it, please."

I gave her a brief rundown of what had happened. "The authorities have sent his body to the Oregon State Medical Examiner in Portland for examination."

"Was he murdered?"

"It looks like it, yes. I think he stumbled onto a horse rustling operation over here in a place called Kiger Gorge. One of the local bad guys—not yet sure which one—killed him to protect his horse stealing operation."

"God, how bizarre. Was he shot?"

"Yes, he was, but they haven't found the gun yet."

"Has someone been arrested?"

"Not yet, but several people are being held for questioning. The chief deputy over here and the local district attorney are sorting things out."

"Was the sheriff involved?"

"Not at this point, anyway."

"When can I get Mike's body back? I mean, we haven't even been able to have a memorial service yet."

"As soon as the forensic examination is complete, they will release the body. I can give you the particulars when I see you tomorrow. Lorenzo is helping me with all of this."

"Maybe now I can cry," she said. "I've been concentrating so much on finding him, I haven't really grieved. Shock does that to you, I guess."

"You can rest easier now that we've found him. I'm so sorry he wasn't alive." I disconnected and turned to Lorenzo. "Poor gal. She's going to be better now, I know, but it just brings back all the horror for her. Will you go with me to arrange for the transfer of the body to a mortuary? I can't let her do this on her own."

"Of course. Before we pack up and leave, though, I'd like to go see Antonio Arriaga, to run all of this by him to see if he can add anything. He'll like to know the outcome, since he saved us from that bunch of bullies at the old barn a couple of weeks back."

"Sure," I said.

"Besides," Lorenzo said, "Antonio and his men spend a lot of time on the mountain and the surrounding area. Not much goes on out there that they don't know about. They might have turned up something that will help us."

CHAPTER 39

THE ARRIAGA SHEEP RANCH was located on the other side of the mountain, right on the edge of the Alvord Desert. As we drove into the circular driveway, five dogs raced alongside the car, barking and wagging their tails. Ahead we saw a two-story house, with a porch extending across the front. Several other houses faced the driveway and a longer building toward the back, with the sign "Sheepherders report here" over the door, sat near two tall barns. I could hear the bleating of the sheep in the distance.

Antonio Arriaga bounded down the steps to greet us as soon as Lorenzo turned off the engine. He embraced Lorenzo and patted him on the back. "Welcome, *mi amigo.*" He shook my hand. "Nice to see you again, *señor.*"

He motioned for us to follow him into the house. The living room was spotless and filled with antique sofas and tables and Indian rugs over a polished oak floor. "Please sit," he said.

A woman walked through a door and stopped.

"Coffee, please, Maria, and some sweets."

After the woman had left, Arriaga explained that she was his housekeeper and his mother's companion.

Maria returned carrying a tray containing steaming cups of coffee and a plate of cinnamon rolls.

"*Gracias*, Maria."

He turned to us. "Gentlemen, please eat."

Lorenzo and I helped ourselves to the refreshments.

"But you didn't come out here to eat goodies and drink coffee with me," Arriaga said. "What did you want to talk to me about, my friend?"

"When we last saw you in the old barn, I told you about Tom's missing friend and our suspicion that the Whites had something to do with it. You said you'd see if you heard or saw anything to help us."

"I remember," said Arriaga. "Has your friend turned up?"

"Yes, I found his body in a cave in Kiger Gorge yesterday," I replied.

"I'm sorry to hear that."

Lorenzo told Arriaga about the horse rustling operation and the Arab man and his interest in the stallion.

"That son of a bitch Dickson White would sell his grandmother to make an extra buck. He's already the richest man in southeastern Oregon. Can the D.A. make a charge stick? I know White. He'll spend whatever it takes to clear himself or his rotten son of whatever he's charged with."

"Both Whites and Clay Murchison are in custody, but none of their guns match the bullet that was removed from Mike Tateman's skull," said Lorenzo.

"What kind of guns?"

"According to Hank French, they were all .45 Long Colt pistols," I said. "Somewhere, there's got to be a 45 lying around."

Arriaga thought for a moment, then stood up. "Come with me."

He led us out the door, down the steps, and across the yard to the second barn. One of the dogs ran along with us, jumping up and around Arriaga as he walked. We entered, and he headed for a large wooden box that was sitting on the side.

He knelt down and rubbed the dog's head and ears. "This is Finder. Since he was a pup, he's always brought all kinds of stuff to the ranch house, mostly from the Alvord. Like a cat does with mice, you know, kind of like leaving a gift at your door."

Arriaga lifted the lid and pulled an object wrapped in a gunnysack. "He brought this in yesterday morning. I didn't look at it very closely at the time because so much stuff turns up out here that nothing seems unusual anymore. I didn't know you were looking for anything but your friend, and then I got busy. Sorry, but this may be what you are looking for."

Arriaga pealed back the folds of the burlap to reveal a rifle. "This is a .30/.30 Winchester," he said. "Most ranchers carry them in their pickups. Seems like you've been looking for the wrong kind of gun. It doesn't have a lot of velocity if fired from far away, but it would easily go through a skull at close range. That means your friend was killed by someone standing close by. The son of a bitch who killed him probably tossed it from the top of Steens Mountain, figuring that no one would ever find it."

"How in the hell could your dog drag it here?" I asked.

"He's pretty determined when he finds something," said Arriaga. "Something this long would be a special challenge, but I'm sure he just kept dragging and dragging."

Both Lorenzo and I nodded in agreement. Lorenzo put the rifle back in the gunnysack and picked up the parcel.

"There might be a fragment of a fingerprint on this," he said, "although a ballistics test will give us the killer."

Finder looked at his master and whined, waiting for praise.

"Good boy, Finder. Very good boy."

EPILOGUE

BURNS RANCHER NOT GUILTY AS HIS SON SENTENCED TO DEATH

by Jeff Walls

Burns cattle rancher Dickson White was found not guilty in the death of a Portland attorney earlier this year on Steens Mountain. During the week-long trial, famed New York attorney J. Raymond Tracy produced evidence implicating White's son, Dickson White Jr., and Deputy Sheriff Clay Murchison in the murder. Both the younger White and Murchison were represented by a public defender after the senior White refused to post bail or pay for an attorney for his only son. "The boy has to stand on his own two feet," White Sr. said earlier in the trial.

Authorities could find no motive for the killing and surmised that Michael Tateman came across an illegal cattle operation in the Steens Mountain area. Neither the younger White nor Murchison took the stand in their own defense.

Both men were found guilty in a separate trial, after hair found on the Tateman's body matched that of the younger White. The .30/.30 rifle used in the killing was traced to White Sr., but he produced a bill of sale showing he had sold it to Murchison.

"Given the heinous nature of this crime—a body left in the gorge so long that it decayed—I have no choice but to impose the death penalty," said Judge Rosemary Napier in passing sentence.

White Sr. could not be reached for comment about the outcome of the trial. He is reportedly traveling in Saudi Arabia.